A SWEDISH CHRISTMAS FAIRY TALE

AMANDA RADLEY

A SWEDISH CHRISTMAS
FAIRY TALE

MISSION HIGHLY IMPROBABLE

AMBER TATE impatiently tapped her foot on the carpeted floor of the elevator car. The numbers seemed to be ascending more slowly than ever. She stole another glance at her Tommy Hilfiger bracelet watch. It told her what she already knew: she was late.

It was only two minutes past nine, which ordinarily wouldn't be a problem. Except Amber worked for Bronwyn Walker, a certifiable grade-A demon who was looking for any reason to fire her.

When Amber had accepted the job at Walker Clay Publishing three years ago, she had thought she'd stay with the company for a long time to come. She'd always wanted to work in acquisitions, and becoming the acquisitions manager for the children's department of a top London publisher was a dream come true.

For a while, things were wonderful. She loved her job. She was given autonomy to manage her department and her workload as she saw fit.

Then, one of the managing partners, Jonathan Clay,

died unexpectedly, and Bronwyn Walker had taken full control of the company. With that sudden alteration, the entire atmosphere of the company was turned on its head.

At first, there were small changes like the free coffee machines being removed and the planned renovation of the staff room being cancelled. Soon after, the flexible working program was suspended. Not long after that, half of the marketing department were fired in what was to be the start of a dramatic restructuring and downsizing project.

Bronwyn Walker had a very specific idea of what she wanted Walker Clay Publishing to be: renowned and highly profitable. According to Bronwyn, that meant weeding out anyone who didn't feel the same and cutting any expense that might be considered frivolous.

Such as anything to do with staff welfare.

Bronwyn was a fearsome force of nature from whom no one was safe. If she felt someone couldn't do their job to the level she expected, they were out. It was often joked —quietly and morbidly—that the HR department should install a revolving door.

Amber had already had a few close calls with the axe that was hanging above her head. One came when a newly acquired author started to get cold feet about their contract, another when sales of a newly released children's book plummeted after an unexpected social media backlash.

Both times Amber had managed to pull things back together and rescue the situation. And her job.

In the back of her mind was the knowledge that Bronwyn's son, Scott, was an acquisitions manager for a rival publisher. It was common knowledge that the mother-and-son duo were just waiting for the right time to bring him over, straight into Amber's still-warm chair.

Luckily, that meant Bronwyn couldn't simply make Amber redundant, as she intended to put someone else in the role. Turning Amber out needed to be done properly; otherwise the situation would lead straight to industrial tribunal. Amber knew her rights and had made it clear to HR that that was the case.

But that didn't change the fact that Bronwyn wanted her gone and was itching for a good reason to fire her. She was sure that Bronwyn was keeping a list of small infractions that could be strung together into a convincing argument to get rid of her. Being a couple of minutes late might just be the thing she was looking for. The icing on the cake of small mistakes.

The elevator finally dragged its way to the twelfth floor. Amber hurried out and into the open-plan office, hoping that she wouldn't be seen.

Unfortunately, that wasn't to be.

Amber had entered the office a hundred times before without a single person noticing her. But, of course, the day she was a couple of minutes late would be the day Bronwyn would see her arrive.

Her boss stood outside her corner office speaking with her assistant and immediately saw Amber approaching. Bronwyn tucked her folder under her arm and slowly clapped. The sound echoed around the quiet office, causing others to look up.

"Well done, Miss Tate. You've *finally* made it." Bronwyn looked at her watch. "I don't know which time zone you were aiming for, but clearly not this one. My office. Now."

Amber tossed her bag under her desk and threw her coat and scarf onto the back of her chair. She took an extra second to look down and check that her outfit looked reasonably presentable despite her hurried rush through the city.

Realising she had little time to do anything about her appearance, and, knowing that a longer delay would just irritate Bronwyn further, she hurried into the office.

"Close the door," Bronwyn said the moment Amber entered.

Amber closed the door and quickly took the seat in front of the large desk, which overflowed with paperwork. Bronwyn was looking at her laptop screen and typing. It was a typical Bronwyn Walker power play, making Amber wait.

After a few tense moments, Bronwyn stopped typing and slowly turned to look at her. "I trust we won't have a repeat performance of your late arrival?" she asked.

Amber shook her head. "No."

She knew better than to explain why she was late. Bronwyn didn't care, she just wanted a promise that it wouldn't happen again before getting on with the day. Coming up with excuses was an invitation to ignite Bronwyn's temper, which was the very last thing Amber wanted to do. Sitting so close to Bronwyn's office over the years had been an education in how quickly the woman could turn from a normal human being into an unreasonable, screaming monster.

"Good. I have a job for you. You've heard of Charlotte Lund, of course."

Amber's brain raced to catch up. Bronwyn dropped names all over the place, expecting people to know who they were with no explanation. A displeased glare was the reward for anyone not fast enough to catch onto her trail of thought.

Lund... Charlotte Lund... she thought to herself. *Sounds foreign, maybe?*

A glimmer of recognition twinkled in the dark recesses of her mind. She hoped she was correct as the memory started to surface.

"Yes," Amber said with confidence she didn't feel. "The fairy-tale author."

"The rights for the English-language versions are due to expire," Bronwyn continued seamlessly. "The collection has not been touched for years, and I think they are due for a relaunch—new artwork, new marketing, the works. Obviously, there's a lot of potential with there being so many short stories to work with. I'm seeing a central collection of all tales, a number of box sets, and the individuals, too. Lots of product to work with."

Amber breathed a tiny sigh of relief that she'd been right. She thanked whatever part of her brain that hung onto nuggets of information that could be considered useless. If she recalled correctly, Charlotte Lund was a Swedish author of children's fairy tales. She'd been born around the turn of the 1900s and had published a number of stories throughout the thirties and forties. They'd been hugely well liked around that time and for a couple more decades before slowly fading in popularity. In the UK market, at least.

"The rights are held by Emilia Lund, Charlotte Lund's granddaughter. Obviously, she lives in Sweden. I want you to get in touch with her and get us the rights to reprint. We need those books to be turning a profit, and to do that we need to bring them up to date. We need to make the stories relevant to children today. Maybe an app? Certainly a website, maybe some games. You know what kind of thing I mean. But to start, we need to get the rights signed off. I want you to get the contract signed and get me a plan to squeeze as much as possible out of the franchise within the next two weeks."

Two weeks took them right up to Christmas Day, but Amber wasn't going to mention that. She didn't think that Bronwyn ever stopped working. She wouldn't be surprised if Bronwyn wrapped Walker Clay published books from the store cupboard for her family at Christmas. Or, more likely, had her assistant do so.

"I've sent you the details of the Swedish publisher," Bronwyn said. "It seems Emilia is a bit of a recluse, but I'm sure you'll figure all the details out. Two weeks."

It was a clear dismissal. Amber jumped to her feet.

"Not a problem. I'll get a plan to you as soon as possible."

"See that you do," Bronwyn said, having to get the last word in.

Amber left the room, closing the door behind her. The office staff had an unspoken rule that if it was possible to contain Bronwyn to her office then it should be done so at all costs. Not that it stopped her, she'd gleefully shout through the glass door. But the impression of a safety shield between the older woman's blistering temper and the innocent souls who inhabited the space outside was appreciated by all.

Amber walked back to her desk and flopped into her chair. A meeting with Bronwyn was no way to start the day, although she'd had many worse meetings with her.

"What did the dragon want?" Tom asked from the desk opposite hers.

Tom worked in non-fiction acquisition and somehow managed to keep out of the line of fire. Probably something to do with his cheeky little smile and habit of complimenting Bronwyn on her questionable ideas.

"She wants to get the rights to some old fairy tales." Amber booted up her computer.

"Oh, the Charlotte Lund thing?"

Her eyes snapped up. "How do you know about that?"

It wasn't anything to do with Tom's area of expertise, so the fact he'd heard about it was bad news.

"Peter in major accounts was on the case for a couple of months, until he was let go," Tom explained, confirming her suspicions.

"Fired, Tom. Call it what it was," she told him.

Tom shrugged, not caring about anyone else's fate as long as he was safe and secure in his boring job that no one really understood or cared about. Tom rarely had enough work to fill his days but had perfected the art of looking busy. That and the endless sucking-up to Bronwyn meant that he was safe from the firing line for a while longer.

"What happened?" Amber asked.

The fact that the project had been with major accounts before being reassigned to Amber wasn't a good sign. Bronwyn wasn't in the habit of explaining herself, so Amber was left to pick up scraps of gossip to find out why Peter had been working on the project with seemingly nothing to show for it.

"Well, I heard that the woman who owns the rights, the granddaughter, is completely off the grid. No phone, no internet. Lives out in the sticks on her own. She has an agent, but he refuses to do anything without her approval, and no one can talk to her so that's not going to happen." Tom swiped a pen off his desk and used it to gesture to Amber. "Might as well get packing."

Amber glared at him. He delighted in making jokes about who was next to find themselves unemployed. He had as much empathy as the pen he waved in her face.

He chuckled and went back to work. She pulled her chair closer to her computer and eagerly waited for it to finish booting up so she could get to her emails and start on what now seemed an impossible task.

"Oh, I think Peter left a copy of the Lund collection, all the fairy tales, in the stationery cupboard. Unless someone's nicked them," Tom added.

Amber flew to her feet and marched across the office to the large cupboard. Since things had been going to hell at Walker Clay, so had people's ethics. If it wasn't nailed down, it usually went missing within a couple of days.

As she went, Amber considered that it would be an interesting science experiment to monitor people's moral downfall when their livelihoods were suddenly in the hands of a madwoman. Interesting *if* it wasn't real life and so desperately depressing.

She opened the door and walked into the room. The formerly neat shelves looked like they had been ransacked during a zombie apocalypse, the result of Sarah, the former office junior, having been made redundant.

Amber lifted up half-empty boxes and old marketing posters as she searched the cupboard. Right at the back, in a darkened corner, she saw an archive box with the lid not quite on properly. She pulled the box out. Around fifty or sixty beautifully designed children's books were lined up neatly in the box, the spines all baring the name Charlotte Lund.

Amber was relieved they were still there, though she knew it was presumably only because of the weight of the box. She replaced the lid and took the collection back to the relative safety of her desk.

2

LONDON CALLING

AMBER SQUINTED at her monitor as she read the tiny writing from the scanned documents. It had been a while since Walker Clay had done anything meaningful with the Lund collection.

They'd sold very well in the seventies and eighties, both as individual stories and in a large, decorative box set. But Walker Clay had done nothing further with the collection, and so it soon fell out of favour with the buying public.

She picked up one of the books on her desk and had a look at the thin, square hardback. The cover and design were dated but beautiful. It was obviously Scandinavian in design and felt like it had come from the turn of the last century rather than from the thirties. The simple illustrations were sparsely decorated in a watercolour style that she knew wouldn't appeal to the readers of today.

She checked out Lund's sales figures around the world. Copies were selling everywhere except the UK, where Walker Clay had stopped pushing them. Though, she could see why. The British market wasn't one for nostalgia. New and exciting were the order of the day. Where some countries were happy to *make do and mend*, Britain had lost that mentality soon after the hardships of the War. Vast consumerism had taken over the country in the 1970s, and the movement had grown stronger with each passing decade.

Cute books that looked like they belonged on your great-grandmother's shelf were not *in*. And people wanted things that *were* in.

She opened the book and flipped through the pages. Like a few of the others she had looked at, it seemed that the translation was off in a few places. Some of the words didn't seem quite right, and the occasional sentence didn't exactly make sense. Something that would never have happened these days.

Her phone rang. She looked up and saw a long number of the screen, denoting an incoming international call.

"Amber Tate," she answered.

"Hello, this is Stine Persson, you emailed our office about the Charlotte Lund collection?"

Amber detected only a slight accent and breathed a sigh of relief that Stine's English was so good. Often when dealing with translation rights she had found herself trying to have a conversation with someone who spoke no English whatsoever. It was always a gamble when taking on these kinds of projects.

"I did, yes! Thank you so much for calling me back. I understand that you hold the rights for the original Charlotte Lund collection?"

"That's right, we manage all the Nordic languages from this office. You're looking to reacquire the English rights, yes?"

"We are. I think I need to speak to Emilia Lund, Charlotte's granddaughter, for that, is that right? I tried her agent, but—"

Stine's laughter cut her off. "Magnus is in his nineties. He was Charlotte's agent, and Emilia never replaced him."

"Wow, so… there's no point in talking to him then?" Amber picked up her pen and swiped through Magnus' name and contact details that she'd written on her notepad.

"None," Stine agreed. "You'll need to speak directly with Emilia. But that is not easy, she doesn't really speak to anyone. Not even to us."

Amber had found some articles in Swedish newspapers regarding the elusive Emilia Lund. Google Translate had thrown up words like *hermit*, not a good sign.

"Yes, I'd heard that she is hard to get hold of," Amber admitted.

"Very. She lives just outside of Malmö, in the south of Sweden. She doesn't have a telephone, landline or mobile. And no access to the Internet either. We send her royalty cheques by post and also communicate by post if we need to. I can provide you with that address if you like?"

"That would be great." Amber jumped on the offer. She'd read some of Peter's notes and quickly realised that getting hold of Emilia Lund was going to be very hard work. While unusual, a home address to send a letter was a great start.

Stine gave her the address, helping with the spelling

and telling her which letters had dots and circles above them. Amber didn't want to get off on the wrong foot by writing an o when an ö was required. She knew from experience that the smallest variation could change a word's meaning, and she had no desire to insert an unsavoury word into the middle of Emilia Lund's home address.

"Good luck, she's not… easy to deal with," Stine said.

"It sounds it," Amber confessed. "Thank you so much for all of your help."

She ended the call and looked at the address she had jotted down on her notepad. She'd been to Malmö once before, on a weekend trip with an ex-girlfriend who wanted to see a concert being held there.

It was a modern city, a little industrial, but still firmly rooted in present. It had trams and excellent mobile service. Every bus stop she saw had real-time electronic arrival boards.

So, she knew for a fact that the lack of technology adoption wasn't Malmö or Sweden, it was Emilia Lund herself. The woman had chosen to live her life with no telephone or Internet.

Just the thought of such a thing caused Amber to shudder slightly. She couldn't imagine being without her phone. She was on it all the time, checking the weather, adding plans to her calendar, checking social media, taking photos. The idea of being off the grid was so extremely foreign to her. Certainly never something she'd choose.

"Do you want me to throttle a pigeon?" Tom asked.

She looked up at him, frowning.

"To get you a feather, so you can handwrite a note to Lund… you know, old school."

She glared at him. "Shut up, Tom."

She opened Microsoft Word and started to type in the address from her notepad. Emilia Lund might be stuck in the dark ages, but Amber hadn't written a letter by hand since she was five and asked Santa for a horse. She wasn't about to start again now. Besides, if she did handwrite the letter it would probably be unreadable. Best to leave it to the professionals, in this case to a word processor and a printer.

Her eyes drifted to the date on her computer. With two weeks to go until Bronwyn's deadline, and Amber having to resort to sending a letter through the post, it was looking increasingly unlikely that she was going to complete this task.

What kind of lunatic doesn't have a phone? she wondered and then got to typing.

3

MAKING A DEAL

EMILIA LUND PLUNGED her hands into the warm, soapy liquid and felt around the depths of the kitchen sink for the missing teaspoon she knew lurked there.

"Found you," she said as her fingers touched the rounded metal. She picked up the spoon and methodically scrubbed at it with the scouring pad.

Movement outside caught her attention, and she saw Hugo's car pull up. She couldn't help but smile at seeing his filthy, old car. How it managed to make the journey from Malmö to Copenhagen each and every day, she didn't know.

She pulled the plug out of the sink and wiped her hands dry. She watched as Hugo got out of the car and strolled over to the mailbox at the end of her driveway. He opened up the box and pulled out a handful of letters. She'd meant to go outside and get the mail that morning, but it had completely escaped her mind as it so often did. Sometimes mail could sit in the box for days at a time before she went to check.

She started to measure out the ground coffee in her old but faithful coffee machine, remembering to add a little extra as Hugo liked his coffee to be richer in flavour. The sound of his heavy winter boots walking up the wooden steps told her that it was the perfect time to hit the start button on the microwave.

"Hello!" Hugo called out as he opened the unlocked front door.

"Oh, we're English today?" Emilia asked, chuckling at his thick accent. Hugo had never been very good at English or any other languages. His Danish was terrible, though improving slightly with his new job.

"I need to practice." He poked his head around the corner of the hallway, hopping on one leg as he untied his laces to remove his boots. "Or I will be fired," he added with a grimace.

"Your English is fine," she told him.

"Not according to my boss." He shrugged out of his thick winter coat, scarf, hat, and gloves. "He is very... hard?"

"Strict?" she guessed.

"Yes. See? I need to improve."

"You are fine. You shouldn't be calling your boss strict to his face anyway," she told him.

He walked into the kitchen and held out his arms. She quickly fell into the big bear hug, squeezing him tightly. He started to sniff the air. "*Kanelbullar*?"

"In English?" she asked. If he was serious about improving his English, then she needed to push him to always speak the language.

"Cinnamon buns?" he asked after a moment, presumably while looking for the correct words.

"*Absolut!*" She patted his back and stepped away to finish making the coffee. "If you don't like your boss, maybe you should look for a new job?"

Hugo sat at the kitchen table, placing the mail he had picked up on the surface.

"I like my job, and the economy is good."

"Salary."

"The salary is good. It's just that many of the meetings are in English, and I'm not as good at speaking English as some of the others. I can improve. I've been watching more movies without subtitles to force myself to listen more. And I have a best friend who is amazing at English."

Emilia scrunched up her nose. "Not *amazing*." She glanced over to the kitchen table, a memory of her father helping with her English homework flashing through her mind. She swept it away as quickly as it arrived.

"Better than me."

"That's because you never listened in school," she reminded him. "You spent more time playing in the woods than you did doing your homework."

"And I still managed to get a good job." He smiled cheekily.

She shook her head, got two cups and saucers from the cupboard, and started to arrange them on a tray.

"All the way in Denmark," she complained.

She had preferred it when Hugo was working in Malmö. He had been underpaid and didn't enjoy the role very much, but he was nearby. They had spent many evenings and weekends together during that time.

Since his move to a new company in Copenhagen, his commute had tripled in time and she rarely saw him. He was tired in the evenings or too busy hanging out with his new friends from work in the city across the sea.

Of course, he'd invited her to join them, but she'd never go all the way to Copenhagen, even if it was less than forty minutes by train. The very thought of going out for an evening, in another country, was enough to send her into a minor panic.

She preferred to be home. Her converted farmhouse on the edge of Malmö was all she needed.

"This is from England." Hugo held up a letter.

"You should open it and read it, it will be good practice." She placed some napkins on the tray and opened the microwave to check on the cinnamon buns.

She heard the envelope being torn open and the sound of paper unfolding. She plated up the cinnamon buns, one for her, two for Hugo, and one extra to ensure an even number.

"Well?" she asked.

"I'm reading."

She chuckled, pouring coffee into the two cups and then carrying the tray over to the table.

Hugo's brow was furrowed as he focused on the letter, his eyes slowly tracking every line of text. She sat down and patiently waited for him to finish reading and digesting.

Reading the individual words in another language was one thing, understanding the sentences was another. She was blessed in that language and words came naturally to her. Unfortunately, Hugo struggled.

"It's a publisher, in London. Something about rights." He handed the letter to her, obviously embarrassed that he hadn't been able to understand all of the details.

She scanned the letter quickly before pushing it to one side. She didn't get involved in such matters. That's what Magnus was for. She hardly ever heard from him, and, therefore, she knew nothing too terrible had happened.

He reached for a napkin and a cinnamon bun. He leaned in and inhaled the aroma of the sweet treats.

"I've missed these," he admitted.

"Then you'll have to come over more often," she teased.

He pouted. "You know I would if I could. I'm just so tired after work. The drive is long."

"I know, I just miss you." She didn't want him to feel bad, but she did wish she could see him more. He was one of the few people she saw on any regular basis. One of the very few she actually spoke to.

"You need to get out more, see other people," he suggested. "Maybe get a part-time job yourself? I know you don't need the money, but you could meet some really interesting people."

Emilia quickly shook her head. Employment wasn't something she'd ever consider. She didn't even know if she *could* do it. Besides, she knew that no one would employ her. She had no experience, and she was terrible with people.

"You might find you enjoy it," Hugo added.

"No, I'm happy with the way things are." She picked up a napkin and laid it out in front of her, placing a bun on top.

"You're lonely," he said.

She laughed. "I'm not lonely, I'm fine. Really."

"I worry about you spending so much time on your own." His eyes flicked up to look at her hesitantly.

It was a discussion they had had once or twice before.

Most of the time they were satisfied to ignore the obvious fact that Hugo worried about how much time Emilia spent in her own company. The rare times they had discussed it had led to disagreements and awkward silences. They never argued, it wasn't in either of their natures.

But Hugo had pushed the issue more and more lately, presumably as his concern for her increased. She wished she could explain to him how she felt, that she didn't want to see other people and that she enjoyed her own company.

"I enjoy spending time on my own," she pointed out.

"I know. But sometimes it is good to see other people. People would love you as much as I do if they had the chance to meet you."

He was clearly trying to flatter her. She laughed and took a bite of the bun, choosing to ignore his attempts.

He sipped at his coffee, clearly looking for another avenue of attack. He reached across the table and picked up the letter from England.

"Write back to this woman… Amber. Arrange to talk to her about business," he suggested. "Then you will have spoken to someone new, and I will not say another word about it."

Emilia slowly chewed the bun, considering his suggestion. She didn't want to cave in to his demand, nor did she wish to quarrel with him. She had no desire to talk to someone else, even if Hugo felt it was in her best interests to do so.

The thought of him not bringing up the topic again was appealing, but not appealing enough for her to reach out of her comfort zone.

She realised there was a solution. She could write back to the woman and suggest a meeting in the local village. Surely no one would travel all the way from London to meet her in a local coffee shop. They would probably insist on talking via the telephone rather than flying eight hundred miles.

But she would be able to tell Hugo that she had upheld her end of the deal, she would have reached out to someone. It wasn't her fault that the person had refused to turn up. Especially if she arranged for the meeting to happen very soon, a time that would hopefully be most inconvenient for this woman.

"Fine. I will contact this Amber and try to arrange a meeting," she agreed.

A smile spread across Hugo's face.

"But if she doesn't reply, or she can't make the meeting, then that is that. I will have done my bit," she told him seriously.

He nodded eagerly. "That sounds fair."

She almost felt guilty. The obstacles she planned to put in place meant that she'd likely never hear from Amber again. But Hugo didn't need to know that. He couldn't understand that she was happy in her own little bubble and didn't need social interaction like he did. It was easier to pretend to go along with his negotiation.

She sipped at her coffee, thinking about when to arrange her meeting.

4

AN INVITATION

Tom threw a stack of letters onto Amber's desk as he walked past. He was often away from his desk, probably on the phone to recruitment agencies looking for a new job, if he had any sense. On his way back to his desk he would get her water from the cooler, or pick up the post from the in-tray, anything to look like he had a genuine reason for not being at his desk.

"Thanks," she said.

She unwrapped the bundle of envelopes from the countless elastic bands that the post room seemed to think was necessary. If Bronwyn saw the blatant waste of supplies, she'd no doubt confiscate all elastic bands in the building.

She flipped through the pile, stopping at a hand-written envelope. She couldn't remember the last time she had seen one. The office address was written in navy-blue ink, the font a gorgeous script unlike any she had seen before. She glanced at the postmark and saw the letter was from Sweden. A look at the back of the envelope revealed a return name and address. It was from Emilia Lund.

She quickly tore open the envelope and pulled out a handwritten letter, gently unfolding the thin paper. She squinted to read the text, so used to reading print that she was out of practice at reading another's handwriting. She could hear her mother's nagging voice in her ear complaining about how people were losing touch with the past and technology was ruining everything.

She read the quick note. Frowned. And then read it again. Her eyes flicked up to the corner of her computer to double-check the date. She looked at the letter again and then let out a deep sigh.

"Problem?" Tom asked.

"Emilia Lund wants me to travel to Sweden to meet her. In two days' time. She's given me the address of a coffee shop, and a date and a time." She looked up at Tom. "Who does that?"

"Emilia Lund, apparently." Tom woke his computer by shaking the mouse. "Better speak to Bronwyn."

Amber turned around and peered into the woman's office. She was in, and not on the phone. It was a good time to go and talk to her, not that Amber wanted to. But surely *she* couldn't be blamed for Emilia Lund's weird demands.

She dragged herself to her feet and snatched the letter from the desk. She walked over to Bronwyn's office and knocked on the open door.

"May I speak to you for a minute?"

Bronwyn nodded without looking up from her work.

Amber stepped inside and stood in front of the desk.

There was no use taking a chair and making herself comfortable. She had no desire to be in there a moment longer than she needed to be.

"I've heard from Emilia Lund, she says—"

"Who?"

"Emilia Lund. Charlotte Lund's granddaughter, the one with the rights to the—"

"Oh, her."

"Yes, um, she says that she wants me to go to Sweden to meet her."

Bronwyn lowered her pen and slowly looked up at Amber. Amber held out the letter for Bronwyn to read for herself. Easier to show her the insanity than to try to put it into words.

"I spoke with her Swedish publisher. Her agent refuses to make any decisions or have any conversations, and Emilia Lund doesn't even own a phone," Amber explained.

"Hence the letter from the sixties," Bronwyn said as she read the note.

"I can't phone to cancel, or rearrange… well, I can't phone at all," Amber continued.

"Go." Bronwyn handed the letter back.

Amber took it and looked at her in confusion. Was Bronwyn telling her to get out of the office or…?

"To Sweden," she clarified. "Get the cheapest flight you can, do it in one day. Go and have the meeting. You're closer than Paul got, and he worked on this for much longer. Maybe there's hope for you yet."

It was a backhanded compliment, but it was as close as she'd get to a positive comment from her boss.

"Just make sure you come back with a deal in place,"

Bronwyn said. "I don't want to waste money sending you on a day trip for you to come back empty-handed."

"Of course." Amber backed out of the office quickly before anything else could be said.

Suddenly, she was going to Sweden. She wondered if Bronwyn was desperate for the rights or just desperate to see her spectacularly fail. She supposed that no matter the outcome, Bronwyn would be satisfied.

Sadly, the same couldn't be said for Amber.

5

EARLY MORNING THOUGHTS

AMBER HELD the takeaway coffee mug with one hand and rested her head in the other. She stared out of the huge windows as the sun came up over the airport. All at once, she felt like she'd been up for hours and as if it were still the middle of the night. It had taken her nearly an hour to get across London to Heathrow Airport for her— completely unnecessary—ninety-minute check-in.

Considering how early her flight departed, all of that prep work to get to her flight had meant getting up at the crack of dawn. Now, despite all of the rushing around, she found herself bored and awaiting information on her departure gate.

It seemed to always be the way with air travel: you were either hurrying every step of the way and barely making your flight or left with so much time you didn't know what to do to fill it.

Businessmen and women were strolling around the almost-empty departure lounge. Most had executive, wheeled hand luggage and looked like they practically lived in airports.

Amber felt like she stuck out.

Yes, she wore a suit and she had a professional leather satchel, but she didn't have access to the business lounge, nor did she have a fancy MacBook to tap away on. In truth, Amber felt more comfortable on a Tube train than on a plane.

Some people thought travelling for business was something to aim for, but Amber thought it was something to shy away from. Who wanted to be up before the sun and sitting around airports, wasting away hours that would have been better spent in bed?

Some of her university friends were forever away from home, jet-setting around the globe for their high-powered jobs, but they rarely got to *see* anything. Every moment from landing to leaving was spent in company offices.

Although her schoolmates said they had been to Beijing, they probably meant they had been to Beijing Capital International Airport and a faceless office in the city. Never having really had time to be a tourist.

Amber loved to travel, but in her own time and to the beat of her own drum. She wanted to choose her own hotel and get up when she wanted, to see the things that interested her when it suited her.

Travelling for work was the exact opposite. She'd never deliberately choose to leave Heathrow before eight in the morning, and the idea of travelling to and from Copenhagen, the nearest airport to Malmö, in a day was already making her depressed.

Her flight home left Copenhagen at nine that evening

as there were no flights between four in the afternoon and that time. Well, none with the cheap airline that Bronwyn approved of, anyway. That meant she'd be home well after midnight, which meant that she'd be exhausted the following day at work.

So, while some people might have relished the idea of travelling for work, Amber dreaded it.

The air travel was only one component. On top of all of that, she needed to meet with the reclusive Emilia Lund. Whom she knew nothing about.

Well, she knew she didn't have a telephone, which was beyond Amber's realm of understanding. Who didn't have a mobile phone in this day and age? Okay, so there was a chance that Amber was a little addicted to her device, but no one could deny that the gadget was practical.

She'd thought ahead and considered that there might be a medical reason for Emilia to not want to use digital screens. She'd wondered if maybe she had some weird eye disease that meant radiation from the screen burned her retina.

Unlikely.

But the meeting was so important that Amber wasn't about to take any chances.

Rather than bring her iPad with all the meeting notes, mock-ups, marketing designs, and cover art like she usually would; she'd printed everything out on paper. Her satchel was heavier than it had ever been. It creaked under the weight of half a tree's worth of printouts and example books she had brought along.

She'd rather suffer back pain from carrying a heavy bag than mess up the entire meeting if it could be avoided.

She sipped her coffee and glanced at her watch. There was still an hour to go before her gate was called. There had been no one at check-in, just a row of three desks all manned by extremely happy-looking employees who were clearly more used to being at work at ridiculous o'clock than Amber was.

They'd all been wearing hideous Christmas jumpers in order to raise money for a children's charity, which Amber gladly donated to. She'd quickly gotten through security and into the departure terminal and now she waited anxiously.

She watched the sun coming up in the distance, illuminating the airport employees outside who were racing about their business on various trucks. The lights from the Christmas tree behind her, outside of the duty-free shop, twinkled in the reflection of the window.

She looked at the warped mirror image, considering the timing of this important meeting. Bronwyn would have no problem firing someone just before Christmas.

In fact, she'd probably enjoy it. It would mean that she could give her son his coveted job at the firm, which in turn meant she wouldn't have to buy him a real present, and then Bronwyn could toast the holidays with the knowledge that her dynasty was being built and her position in the company was secured.

Amber knew that if she failed with Emilia Lund, she'd be out. Of course, if she succeeded it wouldn't be long before Bronwyn found another impossible project to hand her. Failure was coming, and so was the end of her employment at Walker Clay.

Now it was just a question of when.

She prayed that it wasn't now. Looking for a job was never easy, but looking for a job just before Christmas was *impossible*. Businesses were in wind-down mode for most of December. No one was hiring. If she got fired before Christmas, the earliest she could possibly get an interview would be the middle of January, when everyone was back into the swing of work.

She couldn't afford to be out of work for that long. London was expensive, and Amber wasn't the best at saving. In fact, she'd recently taken the lonely twenty pounds out of her savings account to top up her travel card because of all the Christmas parties she'd been attending with her friends.

December was such a busy month for her. Most months were busy, but December was packed solid. She spent a lot of time socialising throughout the year, the curse of having big classes at school and then again at university, but December was the icing on the cake. She couldn't remember the last evening she'd spent at home. She'd started to forget what her apartment looked like.

But December wasn't just busy, it was also expensive. It would, without the shadow of a doubt, be the absolute worst time to be fired.

She lived month to month, and Walker Clay had cancelled Christmas bonuses months ago. There was a lot riding on the meeting with the mysterious Emilia Lund. Whether the woman knew it or not, Amber's life was in her hands.

6

BUSINESS IN THE BAKERY

EMILIA ENTERED the bakery and swiftly closed the door behind her. The winter wind was strong and bitterly cold, but, luckily, the snow had held off. She pulled the woollen hat from her head and fluffed up her hair.

She approached the counter, peering at the assortment of cakes lined up in the case. The assistant greeted her, but Emilia kept her attention focused on the cakes.

Of course, she knew it was rude not to return the greeting. She just preferred to pretend she hadn't heard it or that she was distracted by making a choice of what to purchase. Which wasn't the case at all. She knew what she would be ordering. The same thing she always ordered. Coffee and a slice of almond cake.

Why mess with perfection?

She took a deep breath to gather her courage before looking up at the assistant, smiling, and placing her order. She handed over her money, and the assistant said she'd serve her at the table.

It was one of the reasons Emilia liked the bakery.

There were two in town, but this one brought your food and drink to the table, which meant no standing around making small talk while the assistant assembled your order.

Emilia looked around the small space and debated where to sit. She'd never arranged to meet someone in a bakery before. She usually chose to sit tucked away in a corner in case someone saw her and—heaven forbid—wanted to chat.

But now she was meeting someone, she needed to be visible. A familiar spike of panic ran through her.

Ever since a courier had arrived late the previous evening with a note in which Amber Tate said she looked forward to their meeting, Emilia had cursed her decision to offer up a time and location for their discussion. She'd been certain that Amber would decline.

How wrong she'd been.

She picked a table within sight of the front door but not close enough that the draft would bother her. She removed her scarf and gloves and shoved them, along with her hat, into her bag.

She couldn't believe her bad luck.

She'd felt so smug when she had written to Amber, thinking for sure that her plan was utterly fool proof. After all, who would agree to travel to another country for a meeting in a couple of days? Amber Tate would, it seemed.

Emilia wouldn't even go across the bridge to Copenhagen to meet up with her best friend, so why would a complete stranger fly to another country to meet someone in a bakery?

It was all Hugo's fault, she decided.

Well, maybe her own a little as well. But if Hugo hadn't pushed her to socialise, then none of this would have happened. She'd not be shivering with a little cold and a lot of fear in a bakery, waiting for the arrival of someone she'd never met.

She didn't even know what Amber looked like. She glanced around the shop, just in case Amber had arrived early and she hadn't seen her.

I didn't think this through. What if she's here? How would I know? And if she's not here, how will I know it's her when she arrives?

A mug of steaming coffee and a slice of cake arrived at her table, thankfully stopping her descent into further panic. She gratefully wrapped her cold hands around the mug. It wasn't like her to feel the cold this much. She'd spent many winters walking outside without feeling so much as a chill. The sudden drop in her temperature could only be attributed to one thing: fear.

She hated meeting new people. She wasn't even that fond of meeting people she knew. Only Hugo had managed to get through her defences and become someone she was always happy to see. But then Hugo had been a part of her life since she was five years old. He was like the sibling she'd never had.

And, like a sibling, he nagged her.

Mostly to get out of the house more, which was ridiculous. She loved her house. She was happy when she was at home, alone. And what was so wrong with being happy? Being outside made her uncomfortable. Why should she be forced to do things that made her feel uncomfortable?

The only reason she was in the bakery now was because of her conscience. She knew that Amber Tate was on her way to meet her, and she had no way to cancel the meeting at such late notice.

Her plan to trick Amber had backfired spectacularly. She'd happily written to Amber, giving her as little notice as possible in the hope that she wouldn't be able to make it. In return, Amber had returned her letter giving *her* as little notice as possible that she would indeed be attending.

As much as she hated the idea, Emilia had to be at the meeting she had half-heartedly set up. The idea of asking someone to travel all that way and then just not turning up was unthinkable.

And Hugo would have been unbearable if she had cancelled. In fact, there was a strong possibility that Hugo would still be unbearable. Ever since he had started working in Copenhagen, he had become increasingly adamant that Emilia needed more friends, needed to get out more, and needed to leave her comfort zone.

Part of her, the stubborn part, wanted to do just that to prove to him that she could. That she didn't need his help in doing so. Unfortunately, she was as fearful of the whole idea as she was stubborn, and the two parts of her personality warred over the idea.

Her head whipped up as the shop door opened. A woman in her thirties, wearing a trouser suit, unsuitable shoes, and carrying a leather satchel, entered the bakery.

She was clearly underdressed for the weather, and looked around the bakery in confusion.

Emilia smiled to herself.

So much for not being able to spot her.

She took a deep breath and stood up. "Miss Tate?"

Amber looked over and smiled. She walked towards the table, extending her hand. "Miss Lund, it's a pleasure to meet you."

Emilia politely shook her hand, distantly wondering when the last time was she'd shaken someone's hand. Probably when she was a child playing with her grandfather, pretending she ran the local post office. It was an odd sensation, not unpleasant, though she had no idea how long to shake hands for. Was there a required number of ups and downs? Seconds?

The question was answered for her when she felt Amber's grip loosen. She did the same, assuming that she had performed the ridiculous gesture correctly.

"Emilia, please," she corrected.

"In which case, please call me Amber." Amber turned towards the bakery counter. "Can I get you something?"

"No, I'm sorry, I started without you." Emilia gestured to her coffee and cake. Heat grazed her cheeks. She should have waited, she realised.

"Not a problem, it looks delicious. I'm sure I wouldn't have waited either." Amber placed her thin coat on the back of her seat and her satchel on the floor. "I'll get something and be right back."

Amber watched her walk away and start speaking with the assistant at the counter. She seemed so confident. So corporate.

Emilia rolled her eyes and focused her attention on her cake.

She knew business made the world go around, but that didn't mean she had to like it. Or be a part of it.

A few minutes later, Amber returned and took a seat at the table.

"So, Miss Lund—sorry, Emilia," Amber began. "Firstly, thank you so much for agreeing to meet me. I imagine you're very busy, and I'm grateful for you giving up your time, especially so close to Christmas. As I said in my original letter, I am one of the acquisition managers for Walker Clay Publishing. Walker Clay is a small but rapidly growing publishing house, we're home to some of the best—"

Emilia raised her hand, and Amber stopped her speech, raising an eyebrow in confusion as she did. Emilia actually felt a headache starting in her temples, such was her revulsion at any kind of corporate speak. It was one of the many reasons she had thrown her television away years ago. Too many people talking without anything actually being said.

"No, no," she mumbled. "I'm sorry, I don't like all this formal talk. I prefer to get to know people, individuals. I don't talk about business with anyone I don't know on a more personal level."

It was almost the case. It was true in the sense that Emilia never discussed business at all.

"Oh, I see." Amber clearly didn't see but was trying to be polite. Emilia could tell she'd completely baffled her.

"Let's just… talk," Emilia suggested. She hoped Amber knew how, because she certainly didn't. The very idea of just talking was the reason she had her hands clasped in her lap, so no one could see the shaking.

"Talk… right." Amber smiled. It was a terrified, hollow smile. Emilia was sure it reflected her own perfectly.

A mug of coffee was delivered to the table, saving them from the awkward moment for a couple of seconds.

"Thank you," Amber said to the waitress.

She sipped the coffee. "I… I was surprised. I read an article on the plane over here, it said that Sweden was one of the biggest coffee-drinking nations in the world. I thought it would have been America."

Emilia smiled. "Yes, we're obsessed with coffee. Must be the long winters."

"Must be. I think Finland was the biggest consumer, then Norway and I think Iceland. But Sweden was definitely in the top ten."

Emilia was surprised at how easily casual conversation came to Amber. She was equally surprised that the topic was one that actually interested her.

"Where did Britain come?" Emilia asked.

"We didn't make the top twenty," Amber said. "We have more branches of Starbucks than you, though. Per capita, that is."

It was small talk, but it was unexpectedly comfortable small talk. Amber had done the impossible and put Emilia at ease.

Maybe this won't be so terrible after all, she thought.

7

GETTING TO KNOW YOU

INTERNALLY, Amber was frantically switching gears. She had been planning her introduction to the company, herself, and her plans for the Lund collection for the last twenty-four hours, but Emilia didn't want to hear it. Apparently, she would only talk about business with someone she knew on a personal level. Whatever that meant.

She'd been in so many acquisition meetings that she could probably chair one in her sleep, but she'd never been asked to stop during her opening statement and speak about herself *personally*.

Of course, people wanted to work with people they liked, but that couldn't always be the case. It was a fact of life that some people just didn't get along. It was always a risk, but you got to know the people you worked with *as* you worked with them.

But Emilia seemed to want a guarantee that they were compatible before they even spoke about anything to do with business, and Amber wasn't in a position to be able to decline her.

"So, you live in London?" Emilia was asking.

"I do, in Islington," Amber replied.

Emilia looked at her blankly.

"North London," Amber clarified. "And my office is near to St Paul's Cathedral."

Emilia's eyes lit up. "Oh, how wonderful. You must enjoy walking there during your lunch break?"

Amber nodded eagerly, not wishing to admit that she never left the office at lunchtime. Bronwyn's reign of terror had gone so far as to encourage people to bring or buy their lunch in the morning and then eat at their desks.

"Have you ever seen St Paul's?"

"No, I've never been to Britain," Emilia replied.

"Oh, well, you must visit sometime. I'd love to show you around," Amber offered.

"I like it here," Emilia said simply. "My little corner of the world." She focused on cutting her slice of cake into equal pieces with the edge of her fork.

Spoken like a true recluse, Amber thought.

"I don't travel much either," she confessed. Although her lack of travel ambition was down to lack of funds and holiday time.

Emilia looked up thoughtfully. "I always wanted to travel. I had grand plans of travelling around the world. I keep my passport up to date just in case I ever decide to go."

Amber wondered, not for the first time, how much money Emilia might be making in royalty payments. She was the sole beneficiary of her grandmother's books, a large collection that sold well throughout the world. She lived a simple life, one in which it seemed she hardly ever left the house. And she certainly had no crushing phone and Internet bills to pay.

She sat back in her chair to steel herself. Money wasn't going to be a factor in convincing Emilia to do anything. Not when she had a stream of passive income derived from royalty payments.

Amber fantasised about such things like others dreamt about lottery wins. Having something so beloved and creative in your family, supporting your lifestyle, must have been incredible.

She wondered if Emilia knew how lucky she was.

"So, what do you do in London? Aside from work?" Emilia pressed.

A drunken Christmas event from the previous week flashed before Amber's eyes. There was no way she was going to tell Emilia about *that*. She was sure that Emilia wouldn't approve of the parties-and-alcohol lifestyle that she'd slipped into after university and never managed to let go of.

She knew she needed to grow up and settle down.

One day.

"Um. I like movies, I go to the cinema a lot. And the theatre when I can afford it. Luckily, a lot of my friends from university live in or around London, so I can meet up with them quite a lot."

Emilia didn't look too impressed. Amber supposed that someone who preferred spending so much time at home wouldn't like any of those things. She thought on her feet and quickly spoke again. "And, of course, I love reading. But a lot of the time I'm reading for work, so I don't read in my downtime that much."

Emilia chuckled. "We couldn't be more different. I can't recall the last time I saw a movie. And I read all of the time. One of the few places I go frequently is the local library, but, between you and me, that is only to try to preserve it. I fear it may close down if it is not used, and I'm pretty sure that I'm the only person in town who uses it. A bookstore in Malmö send me lists of their new releases, and I write to them to let them know which books I would like. Every two weeks I have a large delivery of books that I almost devour."

Amber noted that Emilia was practically quivering with excitement. She was relived to find something they could discuss, something they had in common. If Emilia was passionate about books, the meeting could possibly be saved.

"That's a lot of books! You must have an enormous library to store them all."

Emilia blushed, apparently realising her exuberance. "I only keep a few. The ones I don't think I'll read again, I donate to the library."

Amber smiled. "So, you give books to the library… and borrow from the library?"

"I know, I know, I'm probably the only person who uses it and I'm single-handedly stocking it." Emilia laughed softly. "My friend, Hugo, says I should cut out the middleman and just operate it from my home."

"That sounds like fun," Amber said. In her mind she was already thinking of the logistics of having her very own library. She'd definitely have a café to sell members some hot drinks and cake. And there'd have to be a book club.

"That sounds horrible." Emilia visibly shuddered. "As I said before, we're very different."

"Differences are good," Amber explained. "Some of my closest friends are completely opposite to me, but we still get on. If we were all the same, then life would be very boring. I bet in all the books you've read and enjoyed, most of the protagonists are completely at odds with each other and still end up working well together?"

Emilia twisted her coffee mug in her hands. "That is true. So you think, despite our differences, we could be friends?"

It was a strange question, Amber thought.

Then again, it was a strange meeting. Everything about Emilia's way of communicating was slightly odd. Amber assumed that it had to do with the fact that she didn't get out much.

She did her best to make eye contact with the elusive Emilia. "You can never have too many friends," she said.

8

MAKING FRIENDS

Emilia didn't want to admit that she could count her friends on one finger. She wondered how many friends Amber had. Lots, she imagined. The woman was confident and easy to talk to. In the short time they'd shared coffee, Emilia felt oddly at ease, something that *never* happened when she was out in public.

"That is true," she agreed with Amber. She assumed there wasn't any number where one would consider they had too many friends, as if fifty friends were perfectly reasonable but fifty-one would be considered utter madness.

She imagined Amber was good to have as a friend. Easy-going, quick with jokes, intelligent, and well-read— all the things that people surely wanted in a friend. All the things she would want.

She couldn't imagine the look on Hugo's face if he came to visit one day and Amber was visiting. He'd probably assume he was in the wrong house and turn around to leave again. Then Emilia would introduce her *friend*

Amber to her other *friend* Hugo. Amber wouldn't have a clue why that was so funny, but Hugo would be stunned into silence.

"Is something funny?"

Amber was looking at her with a questioning smile, and she realised that she had been softly laughing to herself at the mental image she had dreamed up.

"No, just something I was thinking about," Emilia said. "What do you think of Sweden so far? Have you been before?"

"It's beautiful. I came to Malmö for a quick weekend trip a while ago, but never out of the city," Amber explained. "I enjoyed the train journey up here. You have some lovely countryside."

Emilia felt proud that her home county had pleased Amber. The south of Sweden wasn't to everyone's liking. It was very flat and agricultural, which meant that in the wintertime it could look very barren and bleak.

But Amber had enjoyed the views, which meant she was also a fan of the landscape where Emilia took frequent walks. The more Emilia thought about it, the more she knew she could be great friends with Amber. The chat was by far the most positive social interaction she had been involved in for years.

"There's a lake near my home, it's great for walking around," Emilia said.

"That sounds lovely," Amber replied. "Most of my walking is done in the city. We have a lot of green spaces in London but nothing like around here."

"I love to walk. In fact, I don't own a car, so I have to

walk almost everywhere. Unless I cycle, which I don't do in the winter."

"I can't remember the last time I rode a bike." Amber turned to look at the bakery cabinet. "Would it be okay if I got a sandwich? I'm starting to get a bit hungry."

"*Absolut,* no problem," Emilia said.

Amber stood up. "Can I get you anything?"

"No, I'm fine, but thank you."

Amber walked over to the cabinet and started speaking with the waitress again. Emilia watched her eagerly. She was surprised to realise that she was enjoying her meeting with Amber.

Usually, she'd be eager to go home and return to her normal schedule, but instead she found herself worried about time running out. She didn't know when Amber's flight home was or when she would have to leave to get to the airport.

She felt like she was on the cusp of making a friend, but all that was about to be ruined by Amber going home. Not to mention that Hugo wasn't here to see how well she'd been doing. But Hugo was ever the pessimist, he'd probably claim that Amber was only there for business, not fully understanding the connection they'd made.

Another idea started to form in her mind.

Could I? she wondered. *No, no. It would be wrong…*
Or would it?

Despite her initial panic, her last idea had worked out well. Arranging to meet Amber had been a surprising success. Maybe her new idea would be as effective.

Amber returned with a handful of coins in the palm of her hand, looking at them with confusion.

"I'll admit, I'm not great with numbers, so paying fifty-something for a sandwich is a weird experience. On the other hand, I did feel very rich when I got my money changed up at the airport."

"I imagine I would feel like I was paying far too little for things in Britain," Emilia said. "Paying five of something rather than fifty."

"Currency is strange," Amber said.

Emilia had had enough of small talk. She wanted to get straight to the point of her new scheme. The need to convert Amber from business acquaintance to friend was strong, and the desire for Hugo to see her manage it was equally convincing.

But Amber would likely need a little encouragement to spend more time with her in Sweden.

Her palms started to sweat as she put her new plan into action.

"I'll be honest with you," Emilia said. "I don't do business with people I don't know well. My grandmother's books are very precious to me. I grew up with them, and I know the love that was poured into them."

"Of course, I can absolutely understand that," Amber quickly agreed.

"I'm not going to get to know you properly in this short meeting, but I can see that we could maybe work together in the future, if we connected. So, I'd like to offer you the chance to visit with me for a few days. You could stay a while, we could get to know each other and take some walks around the lake, maybe visit the local Christmas markets."

"Oh, well, I…" Amber trailed off.

Emilia quickly took another bite of her cake. She knew it was wrong to try to convince Amber to stay under the guise that she would talk about business with her. She had no intention of ever talking about business—with anyone. But if she could get Amber to spend time with her, she'd probably become a friend and then forget all about the business side of things anyway. She just needed more time with Amber to make that connection.

"I have a guesthouse," Emilia added. "Or you can stay in a hotel, but there aren't many nice hotels near where I live."

"That's very kind of you to offer," Amber said. "I'm not sure if I can get the time off work."

"But surely it is for work?" Emilia said, feeling immediately guilty at the lie slipping from her lips so easily.

"That's true. I'd have to speak to my boss, though. I'm not sure what she'd say…"

"How about next week? You can stay for a few days before Christmas? I can't imagine much gets done in an office before Christmas anyway."

Amber looked unsure, so Emilia knew she had to drive the point home.

"I couldn't possibly hand over my grandmother's beloved stories to someone who didn't understand them. I'd need to know that you knew the meaning behind them all and felt the same way about them as I do. And there are a lot of books." Emilia nearly felt sick at herself for the lies that were so easily coming to her.

She reminded herself that it was all for a good cause. Once they had spent time together then they would be friends. Amber would surely appreciate another friend above that of a stupid business agreement. She'd probably forget all about the contract once they were friends. And Amber herself had just said that you can never have too many friends.

Amber still looked pensive. Emilia knew she had to go in for the kill. She picked up her bag and started to pull on her gloves.

"I'm sorry, I really need to get going. I am meeting someone," she lied. "The offer is open to you, you have my address to tell me if you can come. If you are serious about getting to know me… and the books, of course."

"I am serious, very serious," Amber said. "I'm sure I can swing it with my boss."

Emilia paused in putting her second glove on.

"Wonderful," she said. "What dates are you thinking?"

9

GOING HOME

AMBER STARED out of the plane window into the darkness. She had no idea how she was going to convince Bronwyn to allow her to return to Sweden for a few days next week. It was probably a moot point as Bronwyn would probably fire her the second she stepped foot into the office without a signed contract anyway.

The problem was, Amber genuinely felt she could get Emilia onside. It was just a matter of bonding with the woman and proving to her that she would handle her grandmother's life's work with respect.

It was true that they had little in common, but she still felt like she had enough similarities with Emilia to convince her that her intentions were true. Yes, Walker Clay's ultimate goal was to make money, but a portion of that money would go to Emilia. More importantly, the books would be rejuvenated and, hopefully, attract more readers.

She realised she'd gone into the meeting with the wrong kind of preparation. She had treated it like any other business setting. Obviously, that was never going to be the case when someone like Emilia was involved, someone who never attended business meetings and was more at home in a bakery that hadn't been decorated since the early nineties.

As strange as Emilia's request was, on some level Amber understood it. If she were in control of her family legacy, she'd want to know who she was dealing with and get to know them on a personal level.

But, as the person trying to get a contract signed, the idea of staying with Emilia for a few days was terrifying. She was comfortable enough in her abilities to know that she could remain professional for the length of a meeting, even several back-to-back meetings. But to stay for a few days with Emilia, allowing Ms Lund to question and prod her to check she was suitable for her grandmother's stories, that would be a challenge.

Work Amber and Home Amber were different people. She defied anyone to not compartmentalise their life in some way when it came to their career and personal lives. She didn't know if she could maintain her professional exterior for days, and nights, at a time, all while living under Emilia's roof.

And she'd have to take up Emilia's offer of staying in her guesthouse. She couldn't afford a hotel, even if there was a suitable one locally, and there was no way Walker Clay would pay for one.

If Walker Clay allowed her to go at all, she mentally corrected herself. That was another bridge she needed to cross. She had until the plane landed to come up with something to tell Bronwyn.

Bronwyn Walker seemingly never slept. Emails would arrive in Amber's inbox throughout the night and over the course of every weekend. Phone calls were a common occurrence, too. She knew that her boss would be watching her flight's progress on some online tracking service, preparing to call the very moment the aircraft landed.

Unfortunately, there could be no flight long enough for Amber to come up with a reasonable excuse as to why she had gone to Sweden for a meeting and returned with nothing. Nothing except another request to go back to Sweden, this time for much longer.

She leaned her head back against the headrest. *I'm so fired.*

———

Amber walked through the quiet airport, smothering a yawn with her hand. All of the shops and restaurants were closed, so her chance of grabbing something for a late dinner was non-existent.

It was the second time that day that she was passing through the airport and everything seemed deserted. She knew that in the middle of the day the place had probably been hopping with people, some going on holiday to sunny destinations or even getting away for Christmas early. And here she was, returning from a day trip to Sweden which had taken hours and produced nothing.

To add insult to injury, her phone rang.

She still hadn't decided what to tell her boss. She was

so physically and mentally exhausted by the day that she hadn't been able to come up with anything.

"Hi Bronwyn," she answered the call.

"I take it you have returned with a signed contract and you'll be presenting your ideas to me tomorrow morning? I'd like to get this project up and running immediately."

"I don't have the signed contract," she admitted. There was no need to beat around the bush.

"I see." Ice dripped from Bronwyn's tone.

"She's incredibly reclusive, hates anything to do with business. Which is probably why these rights have never been renewed before. She wants to work with people she knows and likes. She's old-fashioned like that," Amber explained.

"So, she didn't like you either?" Bronwyn's voice became playful, the tone she used just before making a terrible announcement. She'd made a joke about all the weight that people would lose just before she took all the vending machines away.

Either? Amber thought.

"Well, she invited me to stay at her house for a few days," she said, "so she couldn't have disliked me that much."

There was a pause. "What?" Bronwyn finally asked.

It suddenly hit Amber that Bronwyn wasn't the kind of person to allow rights to expire or come so close to expiring. Especially not something that could be relaunched like the Lund collection.

Maybe Paul hadn't been the first person looking into this project? Maybe this was something that had been going on for a while? If Bronwyn was so eager to get rid of

Amber, and she was, then possibly this was her way to do that because it had already proved impossible for others.

Bronwyn wanted what she couldn't have. She was a shrewd businesswoman, but she also had vanity projects that sucked up time and money.

Was this a pet project of Bronwyn's?

"To discuss plans," Amber lied. "We got on well, but she wants a full, deep dive into the proposals. She's not used to business discussions, so she wants someone to explain it to her, over a few days and in her own home. Someone she trusts. She's invited me to stay, but I told her I couldn't commit to anything. Obviously, I had to defer to you."

Amber struggled to keep the sound of her wide smile out of her tone. Okay, so she'd fudged the truth a little. She had no such guarantees that Emilia wanted to discuss plans, but surely after a few days together Amber would be able to convince her? She had a lifeline now. Surely Bronwyn wouldn't fire her if she had Emilia Lund on the hook?

"She wants to discuss it further?" Bronwyn questioned. "At her home?"

"Yes, as I said, she's very reclusive, and she's very old school. She doesn't have a phone or even the Internet, so the only way is to talk to her face to face. We had a lovely lunch together, and she invited me to stay at her guesthouse for a few days to get the rest of the details nailed down. But I told her I couldn't confirm anything until I'd spoken to you. I'll go back and cross the *t*'s and dot the *i*'s if you want me to, but if you think it's a waste of resources then—"

"No, no. I think we should follow through," Bronwyn said eagerly.

"If you think that's the right thing to do," Amber replied, enjoying having the upper hand for once. "I mean, it would save an awful lot of back and forth. I can get final approval on everything while I'm there, and then we can get straight on with the project without having to wait for Emilia—sorry, Miss Lund—to reply to our questions via post. Which is her preferred method of communication, unfortunately."

She stopped by the exit to the airport, not wanting to go out into the cold just yet. She knew she was playing a dangerous game by stringing Bronwyn along, but she really did think that she could convince Emilia. At the very least, the visit would buy her some extra time.

"Do you have any holiday left?" Bronwyn asked.

"Two days," Amber said. Those two days would expire in March, she'd been saving them for the inevitable job interviews coming her way. Now she felt them slipping through her fingertips.

"Well, I'm sure you won't be talking about business all the time you are over there. It might be prudent to use some of your holiday in order to account for that. We'll discuss it tomorrow morning. I have a meeting at eight-thirty, so I'll see you at eight sharp."

Bronwyn hung up, and Amber let out a groan. Her long day was about to turn into two long days. But at least she wasn't fired.

Yet.

10

A REALISATION

Emilia ran from the kitchen window towards the living room and threw herself into the armchair in front of the fire. She hurriedly picked up a book and opened it to a random page.

It was all she could do to keep herself from giggling. Hugo was going to have such a surprise when she told him what had happened.

The front door opened.

"*Hallå!*" Hugo called out.

"*Hej!*" Emilia replied. "*Kom in.*"

Hugo took a while to take off his winter clothes and hang them in the hallway. Emilia sighed at the continued delay, still trying to look like she was casually reading.

Finally, Hugo walked into the living room and stopped dead.

He looked at her suspiciously. "*Vad händer här?*"

"*På Engelska?*"

"What's going on here?" He pointed to her face. "You're looking all…"

"All?" she fished.

He sat down on the sofa and looked at her. "You actually did it, didn't you? You had the meeting?"

Emilia deflated. She reached forward and softly smacked his arm. "I was supposed to tell you that, you weren't supposed to guess."

He laughed. "I'm a good friend, I know what goes on in your life. So, how was it? Was it awful? Was she really old? And boring?"

"It was fun!" she announced. "She wasn't old, she's around my age. We talked, ate together, and she's coming to visit next week."

Hugo's smile vanished instantly. "Visit?"

"Yes, I asked if she wanted to stay here for a few days. She sent me a letter, it arrived this morning. She's coming on Monday and will be leaving on Friday, as we discussed during our meeting. It's going to be so much fun. I'm making a list of things we can do."

Hugo held up his hand. "*Vänta… vänta.*"

"English," she reminded him.

"She's… coming here? To stay?"

"Yes, I've put fresh linens in the guesthouse. I wasn't sure how many towels to use, so I just gave her all the spare towels."

"Are you crazy?" Hugo cried.

"Maybe she showers a lot?"

"Not that." He jumped to his feet and paced in front of the fireplace. "You've only known her for a couple of hours. Now you're inviting her to your house. She could be a… *mördare!*"

"She's not a murderer. She's a businesswoman."

"They can be murderers," he said.

"She had kind eyes," Emilia argued. "And she's a woman."

"Women with kind eyes could still be a murderer," Hugo said.

"Well, Amber isn't a murderer. She's nice. She likes the countryside, and we're going to go for long walks. We are practically friends already. And once she has come to stay and gets to know me more, we'll be very good friends. I wouldn't be surprised if she comes to stay two or even three times a year." Emilia nodded her head definitively. How dare Hugo besmirched Amber's good name. Of course she wasn't a murderer. She was Emilia's friend. Or, at least, she soon would be.

Hugo just stared at her. He shook his head and turned to face the fire.

"It will be fine," she reassured him. "She'll be in the guesthouse. If she's weird then I'll tell her to leave. And if she doesn't… then… I'll cycle to the police station in town and tell them to come and remove her."

"Will you please use the mobile phone I gave you?"

"I'm not sure where it is," she admitted. "It kept making noises, so I turned it off."

"Those noises were probably me texting you to let you know I'm coming over."

"I know when you're coming over, I hear your car."

Hugo let out such a large sigh that the flames in the fireplace flickered angrily.

"Are you angry with me?" she questioned.

He turned around, his expression softening. "No, I'm just worried about you. This wasn't what I had in mind when I said you should socialise more. You shouldn't be inviting strangers to your house."

"Abby's not a stranger—"

"Amber," he corrected.

"Amber's not a stranger," she tried again, wondering where the name Abby had come from. "And she definitely won't be when she's stayed here for a few days and we get to know each other."

Hugo sat on the edge of the sofa. He looked at her intently, wanting to understand. "So, you two really got on well? You must have for her to agree to stay. It must have been some meeting?"

"Yes, well…" Emilia got to her feet and pointed to the kitchen area. "Coffee? I should make coffee." She wasn't ready for Hugo to quiz her. Yes, the meeting was successful but not in the way Hugo thought. They hadn't suddenly clicked and become best friends.

Hugo's brow furrowed. "Em?"

"Hmm?" She hurried away.

"What did you do?" he asked, following her into the kitchen.

"What do you mean?" She flung open the cupboard doors and started gathering everything she needed for coffee.

"You're not telling me something," he said, standing behind her. She could feel his stare burrowing into the back of her head.

"There's lots of things I don't tell you, Hugo," she said. "I had an egg for lunch, you didn't know that. I'm not such an open book."

"And now you're rambling."

She lowered the coffee scoop into the dark grounds. She knew she'd been busted. It was just a matter of time before Hugo wheedled it out of her. She may as well come clean now.

"I might have suggested we could talk more about business, about the English rights to Grandmother's books, while she stayed here."

Hugo's eyes widened. "You didn't…"

"What? It's not that big a deal. She'll forget all about that when she comes here and gets to know me. We really did connect. I feel like we're going to be good friends in no time."

She felt guilty for causing Hugo's disappointed look. She knew she had done wrong, even if she was great at justifying it to herself. Deep down she knew she had manipulated Amber.

"Em…" Hugo finally breathed out.

"I know, I know," she confessed. "It's just, things *were* going well. We clicked. And then I knew she'd be going soon, and I didn't know how to get her to stay and then I had this stupid idea."

She braced herself against the kitchen countertop.

"I'm a bad person," she announced.

"You're not a bad person," he said. "Just lonely and in need of company. But this isn't the way to go about it."

"I know." She felt a weight lift from her at finally being honest. As much as she had almost convinced herself that she had done the right thing, at the back of her mind she knew it was wrong.

Part of the reason she had been so determined to convince herself that she hadn't done anything wrong was because she knew it was too late to fix things now. Amber was on her way. No letter would reach her in time. And she'd started the ball rolling by lying that she would even consider talking about business matters. To pull out now would include the enormous embarrassment of admitting to that lie.

"You have to tell her," Hugo said.

"It's too late, she has a morning flight."

"Call her? Use my phone if you really can't find yours," he offered.

She *had* found her phone, under the bed and covered in dust. She'd put it on the bedside table and reminded herself to find the cord to charge it up. In hindsight, she realised it was a peace offering to Hugo. *I did this terrible thing, but on the bright side I found my phone.*

"I don't know her personal number. Only the office's and they'll be closed." Not to mention the very thought of making a telephone call was enough to quicken her heart rate.

Hugo nodded. He stared at the floor as he tried to come up with a solution.

Emilia wondered how things had gone so wrong so quickly. She'd gone from not wanting to meet Amber at all to desperately wanting to prove both to Hugo and herself that she was capable of making a friend. She still genuinely believed that she could be friends with Amber. There was a connection between them that she'd never felt before. Of course, that might have been because she rarely saw anyone else to have a connection with these days.

Or because Amber was there on business and was showing her best side.

She rubbed her face. "This is a disaster."

"No, we can fix this," Hugo reassured. "She's on her way, there's nothing you can do to stop that. So, once she is here you have two choices. One, you talk about business with her. Or two, you tell her quickly that you're not interested in talking about business with her so she can decide if she wants to go home."

Neither solution sounded appealing, but she knew that he was right. She couldn't keep Amber in her home under false pretences.

"You're right," she agreed. "I need to decide which of those is the lesser of two evils."

11

PREPARING FOR SWEDEN

AMBER WALKED down the steps of the theatre and into the cold night air. She turned and waited for her friend Caroline to catch up to her. Most of the old London theatres had been built many years ago and then retro-fitted to absorb the hundreds of theatregoers who attended each night. That meant that the small doorways and corri-dors had never changed, and getting out of the building after a performance was usually akin to an endurance test.

After a few moments, Caroline was ejected from the building. Somehow, she'd found herself stuck between two groups of old people who all wanted to walk together while chatting about the musical. As they exited the main doors, she pulled herself free of the crowd and rushed over to Amber.

"Wow, I thought I'd never see the outside again," Caroline joked.

"Why do we always go to the theatre in the winter? There are so many people who don't usually go and have no idea of theatre etiquette," Amber complained.

"Deals." Caroline looped her arm through Amber's, and they started to walk up the street towards Covent Garden. "Money-off deals. We're both poor, remember?"

"True," Amber agreed. "I'm just fed up with sitting next to people who have brought in a paper bag of boiled sweets and proceed to rustle the bag throughout the show."

"That's nothing. The woman next to me had a small bottle of wine from M&S that she got out of her jacket pocket." Caroline laughed. "Honestly, I know they struggle to fill the seats in the winter, especially at Christmas what with the pantomimes going on, but there needs to be an entrance exam before people are allowed into the theatre."

"Agreed." Amber chuckled. She knew to passers-by they must have sounded terribly snobby, but they weren't as bad as all that. They had just had enough of paying eighty pounds per ticket only to have the show ruined by people with no manners.

"Obviously, we're having a glass of wine to debrief." Caroline led them into a busy wine bar.

It was noisy, and Amber winced at the sound of Christmas tunes and multiple conversations turning into a loud din.

"There's an upstairs," Caroline said, indicating a metal staircase with a nod.

Amber gestured for her to lead the way. They cut through the crowd and up the stairs. It was already much quieter on this top floor, but Caroline continued walking into another room. Finally, the ambient sound was at a level Amber could cope with.

"This is nice," she admitted as she scoped out the location.

"Local knowledge." Caroline tapped the side of her head with a finger.

They started to remove their coats and winter wear at a booth with a window that overlooked the busy street below.

"Being a lush," Amber corrected with a wink.

"Rude. And, for that, you can buy me a drink." Caroline plopped herself down on the leather bench.

Amber grabbed her purse out of her bag and went over to the quiet upstairs bar. She was thankful for Caroline's local knowledge. Otherwise she'd never have stepped foot in the busy bar. Even if the knowledge was gathered from many, many nights out on the town.

Of course, Amber went out drinking with friends more often than she probably should have, but that was the way in London. Britain had a pub and bar culture like no other country, and the millions of workers in London embraced the lifestyle morning, noon, and night.

She was served quickly and took two glasses of red wine back to the table.

"By the way, I'm not going to be able to come to your work Christmas party after all," Amber apologised as she sat down.

"Oh?" Caroline took a sip of wine.

"Yeah, work thing."

Caroline raised an eyebrow. "Nope."

Amber tried to keep her expression neutral but felt panicked. Caroline always did this. Somehow, she could read exactly when Amber was trying to hide something.

"Sorry?" she asked.

"You're lying to me. If it was a work thing then you would have complained about it the moment I saw you after work. You would have been all, 'That bitch Bronwyn is making me work,' but you didn't do that. You've left it to the very last moments of the evening, which means you're trying to hide something."

Amber took a sip of wine before pushing her glass to one side.

"Okay, you're right… I just know you're going to tell me I'm being crazy."

Caroline looked positively gleeful. "Spill."

Thankfully, Caroline already knew that her employment was hanging by a thread and that she desperately needed to keep her job. Amber took a deep breath and quickly summarised the situation. She talked about going to see Emilia, their weird meeting in the bakery. Then she explained Emilia's desire to get to know people she planned to do business with, and her agreement to go and visit her again.

Caroline swirled her wine silently for a few moments. "So… you're going to Sweden to stay in some recluse's barn for a week?"

"I wouldn't put it like that," Amber argued.

"Thousands would," Caroline said. "Are you insane? You don't know this woman at all except to know that she lives off the grid. Come on, Amber. The very phrase 'off the grid' was invented to describe those nutcases in movies who murder people."

"She doesn't seem like that, she seems nice."

"Oh, good. Okay, you have my blessing." Caroline snorted a laugh. "I'll tell the police, 'She said that she seemed nice… How many pieces did you find her body in, officer?'"

Amber leaned back on the bench. "Maybe she is a murderer, maybe she isn't. I don't have much choice in the matter. I have to go, Bronwyn thinks I'm close to signing a deal. I'll never sign a deal unless I go back to Sweden. And if I don't sign a deal, I'll lose my job."

"You're going to lose your job anyway," Caroline reminded her.

"Yes, but this way I don't lose my job until next year. No one is hiring now. I need to wait until the middle of January when new jobs are being advertised and I can apply for interviews and stuff. If I'm fired now, there is zero chance of me getting a job between now and then." Amber took a hefty swig of wine.

Caroline regarded her for a moment. "Well, being out of the country for a week should save you from being fired, but you either need to come back with a signed contract or hope that Bronwyn will believe you if you lie about it to survive Christmas and New Year. Of course, this is all theoretical, as Recluse Lady may kill you in your sleep."

Amber shivered. She wasn't one hundred percent comfortable with the idea of living in Emilia's guesthouse as it was. She didn't know the woman at all. She'd seemed okay during their short meeting, but that didn't mean Amber wanted to go and stay with her for any period of time. *What I do for my career*, she thought solemnly.

"I just need to convince Emilia that I'm the right person to work with. That I'll take care of her grandmother's books and legacy. If I can do that, she *will* sign the contract and everything will be fine."

"And how do you propose to do that?" Caroline asked.

"No idea. She seems to like walks, the countryside, not talking to people, books, and her house." Amber listed the woman's hobbies on her fingers.

"Well, you like books," Caroline said, "but the others… yeah, you're total opposites."

"I'm screwed, aren't I?"

"Possibly. Unless you somehow manage to convince her that business isn't evil and you're the right person to work with. Which, considering what you just said, is unlikely. If I were you, I'd just enjoy a week in Sweden. Think of it as a holiday. Maybe work on your LinkedIn profile while you're there. You know, by candlelight. With a quill."

Amber made a face at her. "She's a recluse, but I'm pretty sure she has electricity."

"Do you *know* that?" Caroline asked.

Amber opened her mouth and then closed it again. She didn't know that, but she hoped it was the case.

"Did you ask if she has running water?" Caroline giggled.

"She must do, she offered to cook dinner tomorrow when I arrive. You need water to cook a meal," Amber said.

"Unless she's foraged for nuts and berries." Caroline smirked as she took another sip of wine.

"I don't know why I talk to you." Amber shook her head.

"You like me," Caroline said assuredly. "And I like you. Which is a shame, I'll miss you when you've been murdered. Can I sing at your funeral?"

Amber couldn't help but laugh.

"Sure, why not?"

WELCOME TO THE FARM

AMBER DROVE ONTO THE NARROW, bumpy track and hoped that the inbuilt satellite navigation system was accurate. It was starting to get dark, and the shadows of the trees in the setting sun and the absence of any street lighting weren't helping her anxiety levels.

She'd spent the entire flight wondering if she was doing the right thing. Caroline's words from the night before had stayed with her. Maybe Emilia was a murderer. Maybe she was driving to her doom.

Then again, she knew staying in the office would have presented a different kind of doom. A short and shouty kind of doom.

The car bounced wildly no matter how slowly she drove down the unfinished road. She could see some lights up ahead through the cover of trees. She hoped it was Emilia's home and not someone else's.

So far, everyone she had met in Sweden spoke good English, but she didn't want to test that theory by driving up to a stranger's house.

As she edged closer, she could make out a small, two-story building covered in wooden slats painted in the traditional red she had seen elsewhere in Sweden. She noticed white framed windows with warm, yellow lights shaped like stars twinkling in each one. Christmas decorations, she assumed.

The track wrapped around the building and into a courtyard. The first building she had seen from the track was to her left. A front door and a wooden porch decorated in popcorn lights led her to believe that it was the main house. In front of her was a single-story building also painted in the deep red. It looked like a barn that hadn't been used for many years.

To her right was a much smaller building. It was of a similar design to the main house, but the porch light was a normal glass shade hanging from the ceiling. There were no festive lights in the windows.

When Emilia walked out of the cheery-looking main house, Amber let out a sigh of relief. She got out of the car and smiled with a confidence she didn't yet feel.

"Hi!"

"Hello," Emilia greeted warmly. "How was the trip?"

"It was good, it's a short flight."

Emilia was looking at the car with a frown. "You… drove here?"

"Yes, I hired a car. I didn't know what we would be doing, so I thought I better get a car just in case. It means I don't have to bother you if I want to go out somewhere."

"I don't drive," Emilia admitted. "I usually take my bike. Unless there is ice or snow, then I walk."

Amber didn't want to mention that she already knew that from the short conversation they'd had in the bakery.

"I don't drive often. I usually just grab an Uber," Amber said.

Emilia frowned. "Uber?"

Amber felt a smile curl at her lips. Emilia really did live in another world. Even people who didn't have the car-sharing service in their locality often knew what it was.

"Like a taxi," Amber explained.

She rubbed her hands together. Now that the sun had set, it was getting bitterly cold. She'd not worn all of her winter clothes in the car, but now she was feeling the chill in the air.

"Let me show you to your room." Emilia pointed to the smaller building.

"Thank you." Amber pushed the key fob, and the boot of the hire car swung open automatically. She grabbed her case and followed Emilia into the guesthouse.

"It's small but should suit you for a few days," Emilia said.

Amber closed the front door behind her and lowered her suitcase to the floor. The guesthouse was simply adorable. A small kitchen, dining area, and a living room with a fireplace filled the open-plan ground floor.

A small staircase led upstairs. Emilia stood at the bottom and pointed up.

"The bedroom and the bathroom are upstairs. There are towels on the bed."

"Thank you, this is beautiful," Amber looked around the small space. "So cosy."

Emilia looked proud at the approval. "My grandmother had this building converted from part of the old grain store. All of this was a working farm many years ago. Grandmother wanted somewhere for people to be able to stay. I like it here, but not many people come to visit."

"Then they're missing out," Amber said.

She suspected that people didn't come to stay because they were never invited. She couldn't imagine someone as private as Emilia freely inviting people over, which led her to believe that Emilia must be seriously considering going into business with Walker Clay.

"So, this is your space and you're free to come and go as you please." Emilia crossed the kitchen and pointed to a key on a hook. "I'll be over in the main house. You're more than welcome to spend your time there. Or here. Wherever you're more comfortable, really." Emilia paused nervously by the door and wrung her hands. "Are you tired, or would you like to see the main house?"

"I'd love to see it," Amber admitted. She was intensely curious about Emilia's home. Concerns about her status as a murderer may well be confirmed or denied by the state of the main house.

They exited the guesthouse and walked around the car in the courtyard to the other building. On the porch was a small wooden bench with a Father Christmas made from straw.

"Cute." Amber gestured to the decoration.

"My mother made it," Emilia said succinctly. It was obviously not a topic for conversation.

They entered the house, and a hallway complete with a large shoe rack and multiple coat hangers indicated that this was a house where outdoor shoes were not worn. It made sense, considering the frequent inclement weather.

Emilia toed off her winter boots and threw her scarf onto a hanger. Amber quickly undid the laces on her own boots and placed them on the shoe rack. The room had white wood panelling along the walls and light grey floorboards. The monochromatic look was completed by pictures in black frames. Despite the stark colours, the room looked homey and stylish. Not at all what Amber had been expecting.

Emilia gestured for Amber to follow her around the corner and into the main part of the house.

The downstairs was large and on an open plan, like the guesthouse on a grander scale. A spacious kitchen area led to a casual dining table, and beyond that was a seating area. Everything was decorated in soft whites and light greys, with the occasional streak of black for balance.

It was spotlessly clean.

Caroline had warned Amber to look out for anything untoward, initially claiming that hoarding was a habit of the murdering kind. However, after the second glass of wine, she had changed her mind to include compulsively clean.

So now Amber was on the lookout for a very messy or a very clean house. She found the latter, but she didn't know if it was truly relevant or not. If Emilia didn't go out much, then surely she had plenty of time to clean.

"You have a beautiful home," Amber said.

"Thank you. It used to be part of the farm my great-grandfather owned. My grandmother and grandfather turned it into a home, and my mother renovated it again years ago. I had very little to do with it."

"You live here. And clean it. Very well, actually. My place is not as tidy as this," Amber confessed.

Emilia chuckled. "My bedroom is a mess, that's why the upstairs is off-limits."

Caroline's words echoed in Amber's mind. *And there's always a secret room they don't want you to go in. A basement or an attic. That's where the last victim was murdered.*

Amber shook her head. She needed to get Caroline's morbid thoughts out of her brain.

"Would you like to take a seat?" Emilia gestured towards the sitting area. "I could make us some tea before we eat dinner."

"That sounds lovely, can I help?" Amber offered.

"No, no, it's fine. I'll bring it over. Please, make yourself comfortable."

Amber strolled over to one of the grey sofas and sat down. She stared at the flames of the fire. She couldn't remember the last time she had seen an open log fire in someone's house. She looked around, noting the sparse decoration and furnishings. It was as if everything had an exact purpose. Nothing was frivolous or unnecessary.

She realised something seemed missing and looked around the room in confusion.

"No television?" she called out to Emilia.

"No," Emilia replied. "I've not had one for years."

Amber balked at the very idea. The television was her constant companion. Every morning she listened to the morning shows telling her brief snippets of news, weather, and travel. Every evening she watched something either from the terrestrial channels or through one of her multiple streaming services. She loved to binge on box sets. The only way the ironing got done in her house was if she had numerous episodes of something to watch as she undertook the task.

Emilia entered the living area with a tray filled with cups and saucers and a selection of teabags.

"How do you know what's going on in the world without a TV?" Amber asked.

Emilia placed the tray on the large coffee table in between the sofas. She reached underneath and pulled out a newspaper.

"This tells me everything I need to know." She handed the paper to Amber.

Amber took the paper and flipped through it. She couldn't read a word of it, but it was undeniably a local newspaper for just the south of Sweden, if the weather report was anything to go by.

She was pretty sure that Emilia had no idea who the prime minster was. Nor the president of the United States. Probably for the best.

She decided not to say anything. If she wanted to get Emilia to like her, and sign the contract, she needed to be polite and understanding. Even if she did think Emilia was clinically insane to live off the grid without any television or Internet.

She took her phone out of her pocket and placed it on the coffee table, glancing at the screen as she did.

Her heart hammered against her ribs. No signal. She was so far out in the sticks that she had no connectivity. She hoped that maybe the guesthouse would be able to pick something up. Maybe if she hung out of the upstairs window she would be able to get one bar of sweet, sweet signal.

"I didn't ask if you are hungry. I was thinking of making dinner at six, is that too late? I can cook now?" Emilia offered. She stood by the other sofa, looking tense and nervous.

"I'm fine, thank you. I had a big lunch at the airport," Amber explained. She edged forward towards the tea tray. "Should I pour?"

Emilia nodded and took a step to sit on the opposite sofa. Amber made tea for the both of them, congratulating Emilia on her variety of teas as she did. She wondered if Emilia was a big tea drinker or if she had purposefully bought a large selection because she knew she'd be having guests. Well, guest.

Judging from Emilia's obvious discomfort, and the fact she had seemed generally ill at ease when speaking at the bakery, Amber suspected that not many guests came to the house.

"I said it before, but you really do have a lovely home," she repeated, struggling for conversation now that Emilia was being stiff and awkward.

"Thank you. I like it very much." Emilia sipped her tea and looked around the room as if seeing it for the first time.

"Well, it's the nicest Swedish house I've ever been in," Amber joked.

Emilia smiled. "And the only one?"

"Well, we don't need to admit that." Amber winked. She sat back on the sofa and crossed her legs, placing her cup and saucer in her lap. "I'm so impressed by your English skills. I tried to learn a few Swedish phrases before coming here, but I won't insult you with my pronunciation."

"It's very common for us to speak English," Emilia said. "We learn it in school, and a lot of our media is in English. Television, movies, music. I watched a lot of television when I grew up, and I read a lot of English books. My grandmother was very keen that I become good at English."

"Well, you definitely succeeded."

"Do you learn other languages at school in Britain?"

Amber chuckled. "Sort of. We're very bad at other languages in Britain, no incentive to learn I suppose. We know that so many people speak English that we don't really need to worry about it. Many schools allow you to choose French or German, but we generally start those languages so late that most people struggle with them."

"I see. Yes, I suppose if half of the world spoke Swedish then we wouldn't bother learning other languages either," Emilia agreed. "I read a lot of English books. Many good books don't get translated into Swedish as there are so few of us and many of us can read English."

"I find that fascinating," Amber confessed. "I'd love to be able to speak another language, but I'm terrible at it. I made my French teacher cry with frustration when I was at school."

"I think the key is to learn young and be surrounded by it," Emilia said. "I remember my mother and father only speaking in English to me for hours at a time. If I wanted to talk to them then I had to do the same. And books, if I wanted to read some of my books then I had to read them in English."

"It's very impressive."

Emilia quickly shook her head. "No, no. It's just… life."

Amber smiled. Emilia seemed to struggle with compliments, something she needed to remember if she was going to gain her trust.

"What did you eat for lunch at the airport?" Emilia suddenly blurted.

Amber replied, explaining her love for sushi and how she couldn't resist eating at the sushi bar she saw opposite the baggage claim area. It was an odd question, and another indication that Emilia didn't socialise very often.

While it may have made some people uncomfortable, Amber thought it was adorable. For better or for worse, Emilia wasn't like many other people. She lived her own life and was in her own world most of the time. And it was a world that Amber was keen to learn more about.

13

CAN'T COOK, SHOULDN'T COOK

EMILIA COULDN'T HELP but smile. Everything was going perfectly, better than she'd ever imagined. She couldn't believe that she had a friend over to stay. That hadn't happened since she was five years old.

Amber was so nice and kind, immediately starting conversations and answering Emilia's questions no matter how odd they might be. Emilia knew that she had a habit of saying things that were a little out of place when she was nervous, which usually led to people giving her an odd look, making her more nervous. It was a vicious circle and one that prevented her from wanting to socialise with others.

But with Amber, things were different. She happily answered any of Emilia's questions and didn't make her feel strange in the slightest. In fact, she was as comfortable talking and laughing with Amber as she was with Hugo, which was something she never expected. Amber had a gift for making her feel comfortable. She didn't know if Amber knew how much that gift was appreciated.

"I feel guilty," Amber announced as she arrived in the kitchen. "I simply have to help you cook."

"You're a guest," Emilia said. She stood on her tiptoes and pulled one of her grandmother's moth-eaten recipe books from the shelf.

"Maybe so, but I can't just sit there and watch you slave over a stove for me."

"It's not slaving," Emilia said. "I love to cook. And there are so many things I can't cook for one, so it's good to have company."

It wasn't entirely true. She was making traditional meatballs that she made all of the time. Although she was now planning to change some of the spice mix in order to cater to a broader palette. Amber had spoken about her love of cuisine—Asian food, Indian curries… all kinds of things that Emilia had never eaten.

Swedish food wasn't the most flavourful. It was focused on being hearty and filling. Meals to fuel a Viking nation in the cold of winter. Spices were mainly reserved for desserts and cakes.

She knew her grandmother had a sort of curried meatball recipe, and Emilia had an entire cupboard full of spices that she bought in the hope of one day being brave enough to try something new. Of course, she never did try anything new. She liked her routine far too much. Why attempt to fix something that wasn't broken?

"I'd still like to help, if there's anything I can do?" Amber queried, looking around the kitchen for a task.

The last time Emilia had shared the cooking with someone, she was a child and assisting her family. As an adult, she'd never had to split the workload. She wasn't entirely sure what kind of tasks to give Amber.

Eventually, she pointed to a cupboard. "Could you get a cutting board from in there?"

As Amber got the chopping board, she picked up a knife from the block on the counter and placed it on the work surface. She walked into the larder and returned with a large red onion.

"Could you chop this into small pieces?" Emilia asked.

Amber placed the board on the countertop and picked up the knife. "Sure, no problem."

Emilia consulted the recipe and started to gather all of the items she would need. She pulled out the frying pan from the cupboard, the meat from the fridge. She rummaged through the spice drawer to get all the seasonings. After a few minutes, she had everything she needed ready to start cooking.

She looked at Amber and let out a soft laugh.

"How are you getting on?"

Amber had made almost no progress on the onion. She had almost peeled it and cut it into a very wonky half. Now she was holding onto the wobbly half and figuring out where to begin with her knife.

Amber started to chuckle. "Okay, I'm useless at cooking, you caught me."

She tried to make a cut and the knife slipped from the onion. Emilia quickly took the knife from Amber's hand, not wanting her to accidentally slice off a finger.

"Why don't you sit and keep me company? It might be quicker." Emilia gestured to a kitchen stool.

"Are you sure? I want to help," Amber said.

"It would be a help to not worry about you stabbing yourself," Emilia admitted.

"Good point." Amber nodded and took a seat on the stool on the other side of the counter.

"I can't remember the last time I chopped a vegetable," Amber confessed.

"Do you not eat vegetables?" Emilia started to dice the onion.

"Oh, no, I love vegetables. Always have. I just rarely cook at home."

"Do you not eat?" Emilia asked.

Amber laughed. "Oh yes, I eat. Three meals a day, every day. I just eat out, or I have food delivered."

Emilia lowered her knife and looked at Amber curiously. "You do that so often you've forgotten how to cut up an onion?"

Emilia had eaten out less than five times that year, each of which had been instigated by Hugo. She couldn't imagine going out to eat so often, it sounded exhausting.

"I suppose I have," Amber admitted. "There's just so many different choices, so much great food. It would cost more to source all of the ingredients to make things than it does to buy a meal. And the convenience of having it delivered to the house is great."

Emilia shook her head and returned to chopping her onion. "I don't think there are any restaurants around here that deliver food. Even the pizza place wants you to go and pick it up."

"Wow, that wouldn't work in Britain. We're a pretty lazy nation."

"You're not lazy, you asked if you could help me," Emilia reminded her.

"I have a good guest face." Amber chuckled.

They continued to talk about all the services that were available in Britain in the name of convenience. Apparently, you could get a taxi to take you anywhere by clicking a button on your phone. And you could buy a pre-peeled orange. Emilia didn't know why anyone would need an orange to be peeled for them unless they had a disability.

It was a surprise to hear about all the differences in their daily lives. Emilia had known that Amber went to work and obviously commuted to an office every day. She thought the differences might end there, other than Amber obviously opting to have more of a social life.

But it turned out that there were so many more differences.

Amber hardly ever cooked. She spent more time out of her apartment than inside it. They ate different food, read different books. Amber loved going to the cinema and the theatre. Emilia couldn't remember the last time she had done either. And she didn't even own a television.

But somehow, they found things to talk about. They laughed and were amazed at their differences. Amber couldn't imagine cooking for herself every single day. Emilia couldn't imagine going into a shop to buy a boiled, peeled egg.

They were from different worlds, but somehow Emilia felt more comfortable with Amber than she had with anyone else for a long time.

Even so, the weight of her subterfuge lay heavily on her shoulders.

She kept pushing it down, trying to ignore the part of her that felt guilty for lying in order to bring Amber to her. She bargained with herself, promising that she would be honest with Amber the next day.

She reasoned that Amber would be tired from a long journey, not to mention unsettled due to being in a strange place in a foreign country. Tonight wasn't the night for awkward admissions. Really, Emilia was waiting to confess her sins for Amber's sake.

Or so she was desperately trying to convince herself.

14

OFF THE GRID

AMBER WALKED around the bedroom of the guesthouse and let out a long sigh. At ten o'clock, Emilia had declared that it was bedtime. Amber had smothered a smile as she watched the Swede hurry around the kitchen and the dining room tidying up following their meal. It seemed that Emilia was a stickler for bedtime.

Amber couldn't remember the last time she'd gone to bed so early. Probably when she'd had the flu a few years back.

She held her mobile phone out and circled the room, seeking a signal. As she had dreaded, there was nothing. She was completely cut off from the outside world.

She'd thought that the two-hour power cut on a Sunday afternoon a few months ago had been bad, but that was nothing compared to having no TV, no mobile signal, and no Internet access whatsoever. At least then she had still been able to use her phone, check her email, and play games.

Now there was nothing to entertain her and she wasn't in the least bit tired.

She sat on the edge of the bed and put her phone on the bedside table. It was like she had been thrown back in time, into a strange world that she felt very uneasy in.

It was a world that Emilia had carved out for herself. Amber knew that Sweden had perfectly good Internet access. They had television, ride-sharing services, food ordering apps.

Sweden was a vibrant and modern country with technology being used for everything. They were the home of Candy Crush, for heaven's sake. It was as modern and technologically advanced as Britain.

But Emilia's little oasis, just outside of one of the main cities of the country, couldn't be further removed from the modern day.

Amber had no idea what they intended to do for the next few days. She couldn't imagine how to fill the time. There was quite simply nothing to do, and she worried that they had already exhausted their conversation.

Emilia was adorably awed by Amber's modern-day lifestyle. Amber had deliberately kept some information back, fearing that explaining things like Tinder would be enough to make poor Emilia implode.

Talking to Emilia was like meeting a time traveller who had been pulled out of the past and had endless questions about how everything worked in this strange, new world.

She opened up her suitcase and pulled out a pair of pyjamas. She'd bought them new from the local supermarket, something else that probably would have blown Emilia's mind.

Nightwear? In a supermarket? Next to the pre-roasted chicken?

She usually slept naked but had decided to invest in some cheap sleepwear considering the cold temperatures and the fact that she was staying in someone else's house. She'd had no idea what to expect and only now realised how lucky she was that things had worked out.

Normally she would never have considered jumping on a plane and staying with someone she hardly knew. The threat of unemployment had caused her to act rashly, but thankfully things seemed to be working out well.

She held her pyjamas in her hand, realising that she needn't have worried about the potentially cold temperatures. While the outside was freezing, both the main house and the guesthouse were toasty and warm. Crossing from one to the other wasn't exactly fun, but it took less than ten seconds.

She glanced out of the window. The main lights in the house were off, but the lit-up paper stars in all the windows remained on. Amber had seen them in other houses on the drive over. Emilia had explained that they were common Christmas decorations, that many Swedish households liked to display candles or stars in the windows during the winter months.

She let out a sigh and wondered what to do with herself. It had been a very long time since she had been well and truly bored. Of course, she thought she had been bored before, but that passed after a couple of seconds. She had access to friends via text, video chat, email, and good, old-fashioned telephone. Games, movies, television box sets, and music could all be accessed as the touch of a button. Boredom only ever lasted a few moments.

That wasn't the case currently. Now she was properly *bored*. She was also pre-emptively bored, knowing that things weren't going to change anytime soon.

She wasn't tired, despite Emilia's insistence that she must be exhausted after her travels. Another throwback to the Victorian era from which Emilia seemed to hail. She acted as if Amber had been stuck on a passenger steam liner for the last week. She'd actually been on a relatively comfortable plane for around ninety minutes.

She tossed her pyjamas onto the bed and then flopped down onto the soft duvet. She stared up at the ceiling.

Part of her wanted to refuse to go to bed so early. It seemed ridiculous. She was a grown woman, she didn't need a bedtime. She went to bed when she was tired. Not when the clock told her.

She frowned.

"Wait a minute," she muttered.

She held her arm up above her face, staring at her watch.

"Oh, no… no way."

She had suddenly remembered the time difference. Sweden was one hour ahead. Which meant, according to Amber's watch and her internal body clock, it was only nine.

She flopped her arm back down on the bed.

"Oh, well," she said to herself. "When in Rome."

She pictured Emilia, presumably tucked up in bed.

Probably wearing an ankle-length nightdress buttoned up to the neck. Maybe holding a teddy bear as she slept.

She chuckled. Emilia may have been a little odd, but she seemed happy with her life and happy to see Amber. While Amber was bored enough to consider going out into the nearby forest and screaming with frustration, Emilia seemed genuinely pleased to have company.

It boded well for the currently unsigned contract. Emilia had said she would only do business with people she liked, and she seemed to like Amber. They had chatted and laughed. The evening had been pleasant enough.

She decided to bring up the subject of the contract the following day. That way she could get Emilia's signature secured as soon as possible and then rest easy. Though rest was the last thing she wanted.

She blew out a frustrated breath as she continued to stare at the ceiling.

She felt sorry for Emilia, stuck out in the middle of nowhere with no one to speak to. She said she was happy, but Amber detected an underlying hint of sadness. And who wouldn't be sad? Clearly the house had been in the family for generations. It was a house that had grown with the family and was built to shelter many people. Emilia was just one person rattling around a large house. She'd be better off in the guesthouse, Amber mused. Less room to fill.

Emilia spoke about her family only through stories of things that had happened a seemingly long time ago. While she hadn't said anything specific, Amber got the distinct impression that talking about the Lunds was off-limits.

The fact that Emilia lived alone led Amber to believe that they had all died. Of course, she knew about Charlotte Lund's death, but knew nothing about Emilia's grandfather, mother, or father. The fact they weren't around, or spoken about, was one thing that did *not* bode well.

She sat up and stretched her hands above her head. She decided to do some yoga in the hope that it would tire her out before bed. Her mind needed clearing, and it wasn't like she had anything else to do.

Standing up, she shook her body as she tried to clear her mind. Unfortunately, all she could think about was the hike around the lake they had planned for the next day. Amber couldn't remember the last time she had only had one thing planned for an entire day.

But apparently that was the way Emilia did things. They were going to go for a hike around the lake, as she'd somehow got the impression that Amber would love it. She didn't go out of her way to dissuade Emilia from the idea. If Emilia would be happy walking around the lake, then Amber would pretend that she was, too.

At the moment, she was in the business of doing things that would make Emilia happy.

Because happy Emilias were apparently the ones who signed contracts. And *that* would make Amber happy.

THE BEAUTIFUL LAKE

THEY WERE HALFWAY around the lake, and Emilia couldn't stop smiling. Everything was going so well. Some snow had fallen the night before and continued to fall intermittently throughout the day. That meant that the walk around the lake was beautifully picturesque. And she relished the idea of showing off her beloved landscape to Amber.

If she'd remembered to bring her camera, then it would have been the perfect day to take some photographs. Although she already had many photos of the lake during all kinds of weather. It was, after all, her favourite place to walk.

Amber had been a little quiet ever since breakfast. Probably still tired from her travel. Emilia didn't really know how long it took to recover from travel, but she assumed quite a while. Being away from home and in another country was sure to be exhausting.

Emilia put her hands deeper into the large pockets of

her thick winter coat. It looked more and more likely that there would be a white Christmas. It wasn't a guaranteed thing in the south of Sweden, but she often hoped for it. The landscape was breathtaking after the first snow had fallen.

Right now, it was a little more than a dusting. The white powder crunched as it compressed beneath her boots. The lake had a thin layer of ice over it. The ducks walked across the frozen surface and occasionally swam in the melted portions.

"I wish the lake had fully frozen this winter," she said. "Then we could have skated on it."

Amber glanced at the large lake. "Skated on it? Isn't that dangerous?"

"Not if it's been frozen a while."

"How do you know?" Amber asked.

"You just do." Emilia didn't know exactly how she knew when the lake was solid enough to support her skates. It was knowledge she had grown up with. It seemed strange that Amber didn't have that sixth sense.

"Do you go skating often?" Emilia asked.

"Never," Amber said. "Never learnt. There's a temporary rink set up near the office, but I've never been. Too old to fall and break a bone."

Emilia laughed. "You can't be that old."

"Thirty-two, old enough to know I can't skate," Amber replied. "How much longer do you think it is until we get around the lake? I've lost my bearings."

"It's another mile," Emilia replied. "Then half a mile back to the house. It's a nice, long walk for cool winter days. I've lost count of how many times I've walked around the lake."

"I bet."

Emilia frowned. Amber was staring steadfastly at the ground. The British woman had been so chatty the evening before, but the longer they were out, the less she seemed to have to say.

Emilia wasn't any good at initiating conversation at the best of times, but now she found herself carrying the weight for both of them.

She suspected that Amber was overcome with the beauty of her surroundings. London could never look as pretty as the lake on a winter's day. And, of course, the travel must have caught up with her. She knew people often suffered jetlag after a long journey.

"I used to walk with my grandparents' dog around here. We'd let him off the lead, and he'd swim in the lake. Only in the summer, of course. Do you have any pets?" Emilia asked.

"No, I'm allergic to cats and dogs. Well, probably just to fur."

"Oh! So, you've never had any pets?"

"No."

Emilia couldn't imagine not having pets. She didn't have any at the moment, except the local feral cat who sometimes walked through her garden, but growing up, there had been lots of pets. She had an entire photo album dedicated to them.

They continued walking and Emilia struggled to think of any other topics. Amber walked beside her silently. Her eyes were cast down, seemingly watching the snow flick from the tips of her boots with every step she took. Her hands were buried deep in her pockets, and Emilia could hardly see her face, her scarf so high and her hat so low.

There must be something else to talk about, she thought. It was becoming obvious that the easy-going conversation flow of the day before had mainly been down to Amber. Emilia knew it was up to her to pick up the slack, and, as she only really knew one solid thing about Amber, she would have to try to talk about work.

"So, how long have you been working in publishing?"

"About eleven years. Three at Walker Clay."

"And you enjoy it?"

There was a period of silence before Amber replied. "Yes, it's a great company to work for."

Emilia wasn't sure, but she thought there was more to the subject than Amber was admitting. But she had no idea how to go about asking.

"Are Walker and Clay names of people?"

"Yes, Bronwyn Walker and Jonathan Clay."

"They own the company?"

"They did. Jonathan died a little while ago. Bronwyn has taken over but kept the name as it was."

Emilia couldn't think of a single other question about Amber's employment. She knew that there must have been hundreds of potential questions, but she couldn't think of even one of them. She supposed it was simply because she had nothing to draw on. She'd never worked, never stepped foot in an office.

She decided to enjoy the silence for a while and listen

to the sound of the wind through the trees and the crunch of powder beneath her feet.

Amber seemed to be happy with the silence. Emilia wondered if Amber was more like her than she had at first thought. She loved peace and quiet. As much as she enjoyed Hugo's visits, she really enjoyed the moments after he had gone home when she was left with the familiar background noise of her own home.

It was at odds with what Amber had told her about herself. She'd referred to herself as a social butterfly, often spending more time out and socialising with friends than she spent at home, so the silence was confusing. Emilia couldn't understand it.

"I was thinking of making a roast chicken dinner tonight," she said after a long period of silence.

"That's very kind of you."

"You like chicken?" Emilia clarified.

"I do."

"Good, it's Hugo's favourite. Did I tell you about Hugo?"

"You mentioned him last night. Your friend from school, right?"

"Yes, that's right." Emilia was pleased that Amber had remembered. "He's the only person from my school who stayed in town. Well, other than me, of course. Then, there were only eighteen of us. Everyone else wanted to live in bigger cities. I don't know why. We have everything you could need here."

Amber hummed an agreement.

Emilia had now completely run out of conversational points. She really didn't know what people talked about all day. Amber seemed to be enjoying the silence, so she decided to remain quiet for the rest of the walk. They could take in the scenery together, enjoy it in companionable silence.

It really was a lovely day.

16

THE BLOODY AWFUL LAKE

IT WAS A TERRIBLE, horrible day. Amber had never felt cold like it. It was the kind of cold that quickly seeped through all clothing, past skin and flesh, and buried itself deep within bones.

She'd never really understood the meaning of cold until now. The bizarre part was, it wasn't even that cold out. She'd checked the temperature before she left, and the weather station in Emilia's kitchen said the same thing— average temperatures for that time of year, like a cool London day.

But she hadn't factored in two things: wind chill and the fact that Swedish cold was a different *kind* of cold. She'd always thought people who said that were crazy. A temperature was a temperature, it shouldn't matter where you were.

She now knew that wasn't the case.

Geography mattered.

Like when her friend Rebecca had gone to New York

completely ill-prepared. She'd seen the weather report and thought she had packed appropriately. Apparently, it was a different humidity level in New York to what it was in London, and she'd promptly gone shopping and bought several more layers.

Amber had never really understood that story. Until today.

Now she knew about different types of cold. Walking around that barren, icy lake had been one of the worst experiences of her life.

She didn't say anything because Emilia clearly adored the lake, and walking. Since Emilia was having a good time, Amber knew she had to put up with things and pretend she was, too.

The entire way around the lake she had been reminding herself of the contract. She needed to keep Emilia happy to get the contract signed. She could cope with some frostbite as long as it meant that Emilia felt they were two peas in a pod and could work together.

She'd also been promising herself a hot shower the moment they returned. But now that she stood under the hot water, she was disappointed to find that it wasn't helping as much as she'd hoped. Several hours out in the cold had plunged her body temperature down so far that she wondered if she would ever feel warm again.

She imagined that she must have looked truly pathetic, sitting on the floor of the shower with her knees to her chest, hot water falling down her face.

She shivered, partly from the chill and partly from the memory of Emilia's constant need to identify every plant or bird call. And her subsequent need to look interested when she was really wondering if she could die from being bitterly cold.

She leaned her head against the wall and closed her eyes. Emilia had occasionally drifted into more personal topics, once asking if she were seeing any 'boys'. She hadn't been asked that since she was a child and a friend of her parents or older relatives had grilled her. Why adults thought it was appropriate to ask young adults and children that question was completely beyond Amber. It turned them into pseudo-sexual beings at a young age and often made them feel as if they needed to be seeing *boys* to be somehow complete to an adult's eyes.

It didn't help that Amber had known she was bisexual, though more interested in *girls* than *boys*, since she first heard the word at six years old. She'd kept an open mind as she'd grown up, but the desire for all genders had always remained. She'd dated her first girl when she was only fourteen, her first boy when she was sixteen. Since then, she'd favoured women but had been in relationships with both.

She'd been open about her sexuality all her life. Living in London meant that she knew she was surrounded by people like her. She read *Honey Magazine* cover to cover every month and frequently saw first-hand how large and vibrant her community was.

Yet she'd frozen when Emilia had asked. It was a usual, though childishly phrased, question. Rather correcting Emilia and explaining that she was bisexual, she had simply shaken her head and remained quiet.

Guilt weighed her down. She had promised herself to never live in the closet. It was sheer dumb luck that she lived in a time and a country where being gay was accepted by the majority. She felt she owed it to those who didn't have that privilege to live an out lifestyle.

And she'd always done so. Until today.

She really didn't know how sweet, naïve Emilia would respond to having a bisexual woman staying in her home. Would she even know what bisexuality was? Amber had met a few people who thought you were either gay or straight. She wouldn't be surprised if Emilia's understanding was as simplistic.

She felt awful. She hadn't lied, but she had deliberately withheld information which pretty much was the same thing. Trying to tell herself that it was a business arrangement and it wasn't relevant didn't help. Passing for straight in order to get a contract was about as low as Amber thought she could go.

Now, on top of the stress of trying to keep her job, and the pressure of trying to make Emilia like her, she knew she had to tell the truth. It would eat at her if she didn't admit her sexuality to Emilia.

She couldn't live a lie.

She knew she was blowing things out of proportion. It had just been an innocent question, but it was an important one for Amber. One that she had been asked time and time again over the course of her life.

It was a question that she always dreaded. It meant that she was always in a state of coming out, usually to complete strangers or business acquaintances, having to admit her sexual preferences to people she hardly knew.

But she did it. Time and time again, she did it, because she felt it was important to do so and to be honest.

She knew that she, unlike so many others, *could* do it. Simply because she was born in the UK rather than one of the many countries around the world where she could be imprisoned or even killed for admitting such a thing.

Not that she ran up to anyone on the street and announced she was bisexual. No, she wasn't in the habit of shouting it from the rooftops, but it was surprising how often the topic came up in everyday conversation.

Now the topic had come up, and she'd lied by omission. She needed to correct that matter. Her moral compass simply wouldn't allow her to ignore it.

Suddenly, the warm water ran cold. Amber screeched and crawled out of the shower. She sat on the bathroom floor, looking up at the traitorous showerhead.

"Damn you," she muttered. "And damn Sweden, snow, cold weather, and Bronwyn Walker." She stood up, grabbed the towel from the back of the door, and swung it around her body.

She realised that she'd not damned Emilia, who was at the centre of all of her current issues. Somehow that felt wrong. Her anger was still laser-focused on Bronwyn. Bronwyn was cruel and calculating. Emilia was just bumbling around in her own little world, none the wiser to anything that went on around her.

Amber looked at her phone. It was essentially just a clock now. No connectivity meant half her apps refused to work, and she always streamed entertainment so not a single song or television program was saved to the device.

It was half an hour until Emilia had said dinner would

be ready. She needed to hustle if she was going to get over there and try to help out. She looked out of the window, seeing snow starting to fall again. Getting from the guest-house to the main house only took a few seconds, but it was longer than she currently wanted to be in the cold air.

"Bloody winter," she mumbled.

17

INTRODUCING... A SWEDISH MILE

AMBER WAS IMMEDIATELY LED AWAY from the kitchen and towards the dining area. Apparently, her terrible cooking skills had rendered her banned from cooking and relegated to laying the cutlery at the table instead.

She thought she'd done a good job, but Emilia's knowing smirk as she brought a dish to the table said otherwise.

Emilia didn't say anything, she was too polite. Instead she offered Amber a choice of fruit juices—apparently wine was only something for Christmas Day.

She chose cloudberry juice because she'd never heard of it before and thought for sure it was made up. Possibly even a cocktail. Alcohol would be a dream come true. She still felt cold to the bone, despite the several layers she had piled on in the hope they would help her warm up.

A nice drop of something alcoholic would warm her up, improve her mood, and take the edge off all the stress she was feeling.

Emilia placed a glass of juice on the table. It looked like watered-down orange juice. Amber took a sip.

Definitely no alcohol, she told herself.

"Thank you," she said. Manners first, even if she was feeling terrible.

She looked longingly at the warm oven to one side of the room, and then to the logs burning in the fireplace on the other side of the room. She seemed to be in the middle of two heat sources which she would have given her right arm to be nearer.

She watched Emilia cooking. The woman looked so happy as she bustled around the kitchen, preparing the food. She'd obviously had a great day and was continuing to have fun. She was also clearly oblivious to Amber's terrible mood.

But she couldn't begrudge her having a nice day. Even if that nice day was the sole reason for Amber's bad one.

Despite Amber's offers of assistance, Emilia served the dinner alone, insisting that she was a guest. Amber wasn't comfortable being waited on, so she decided that she'd have to try to turn the tables in the following days. For now, she was content to eat the delicious-looking meal that Emilia had prepared.

It was obvious that Emilia was an expert chef, presumably because she cooked for herself every single day. That very fact continued to blow Amber's mind. Emilia took cooking in her stride. It was something she had to do every day if she wanted to eat. And she'd clearly become accomplished at it.

Amber knew without a shadow of doubt that if she were forced to cook her own meals every day, those meals would consist of unwrapping something premade. Breakfast would be a cereal bar, lunch would be a bag of crisps and a premade sandwich, and dinner would of course be something that required stabbing and putting in the microwave for four minutes.

But, luckily, she would never have to cook all her own meals. She lived in a city where eating out, getting food delivered, or picking up food and taking it home were a way of life. Often it was cheaper to eat cheap takeout than it was to cook the meal.

She thanked Emilia for her time in the kitchen and for the food and took a bite of the vegetable and lamb stew. It was sensational. She had to admit that there was something special about home-cooked food. Cooked by someone who knew how, of course. If she'd cooked it, it would have quickly found its way to the bin.

"The weather forecast has changed," Emilia said. "Apparently we will be getting some more snow. You'll be able to see how beautiful the landscape is in winter."

Amber's eyes flicked up to the window. It was flat, dark, and tree-lined. When the snow fell it would be exactly the same, just colder and more white.

"Absolutely," she lied. She had no interest in seeing anymore of the landscape. She'd seen enough during her icy march that afternoon.

They continued to eat, Amber remaining silent while Emilia regaled her with stories of all the fun times she'd had down by the lake. Swimming in the summer, boating in the spring, skating in the winter. And endless tales of walks.

"It is a very big lake," Amber commented.

"Oh yes, at least…" Emilia looked up at the ceiling as she thought about it. "Three Swedish miles."

Amber paused. "*Swedish* miles?"

"Yes," Emilia replied.

"Is… is that different to a British mile?"

"Absolut! I think a Swedish mile is around six of your miles," Emilia explained.

Amber felt sick.

When she had asked Emilia how long the walk home would be at one point, she had said it was about one mile. Amber knew she walked a couple of miles a day in London and had wondered how that single mile had felt so damned long.

Now she knew. She'd not walked three miles. She'd walked *sixteen*. In freezing temperatures. No wonder she felt so unwell.

"It is a good workout," Emilia said.

"It certainly is that," Amber agreed, annoyed that she didn't even know there was such a thing as a Swedish mile.

"And so very beautiful. My favourite place to be," Emilia enthused.

"So you mentioned," Amber said. *Several times,* she thought.

It was nice that Emilia adored the geographical feature so much, but Amber couldn't help but feel sad for her. It was as if her life completely revolved around being inside the house or visiting to the lake in order to reminisce about the previous times she'd been. Usually times with her family.

In fact, her stories all seemed to include family members who were no longer around. Swimming with her father, walks with her grandmother. None of Emilia's stories were about the lonely walks she took so frequently took now.

If Amber wasn't in the business of trying to make friends with Emilia, she might have pointed that out. She may have even gone as far as to suggest that Emilia was trying to recreate memories that were long gone rather than attempting to build new ones.

But that wasn't why she was here. She was here to demonstrate that she was the right person for Emilia to entrust with her grandmother's stories, not to try to psychoanalyse her lifestyle.

They finished their meal in silence until Amber asked, "So, what do we have planned for tomorrow?"

"Oh, I thought we might take a stroll through the winter markets. It will be a bit cold now more snow is forecast, but we can just bundle up with another layer or two."

Amber felt a flash of fear. Not that she could admit that to Emilia. If Emilia wanted to show her the winter market, then she'd go and she'd smile the entire way around. Even if her smile was a partial grimace.

She was just about to say how perfect that sounded when Emilia looked at her oddly.

"Or not?" Emilia asked with a worried brow.

Busted. Amber realised she hadn't covered up her expression quickly enough.

"I… I got pretty cold when we were out today," she confessed.

"Oh my!" Emilia's eyes widened. "I didn't know."

"Yeah, I didn't say anything. I didn't want to spoil the

walk. I just can't get warm. I can't really imagine spending the day out in the cold again tomorrow," Amber admitted.

"You're still cold?" Emilia asked, surprise evident.

Amber nodded.

Emilia reached across the table and placed the back of her fingers on Amber's cheek.

"You're freezing!"

Emilia was up from her chair like a shot. She grabbed Amber's arm. Amber dropped her knife and fork onto her almost-empty plate and allowed herself to be dragged over to the fireplace in the sitting area.

She was placed on the end of the sofa, nearest to the open fire. A moment later Emilia returned with a thick, crocheted blanket. She wrapped it around Amber's shoulders and kept her arm around her.

"I had no idea you were cold, I'm so sorry. If I'd known, I would have hurried back rather than showing you where I found the birds' nests when I was a child."

"It's fine, I should have said something," Amber conceded.

The heat from the fire was lovely, and the warmth of Emilia's arm behind her was so soothing.

"I should have noticed," Emilia said. "Tomorrow we will do something indoors."

"Thank you, I'd appreciate that," Amber said.

"You are silly," Emilia said kindly. "You should have said something."

Amber knew it was true, but she suffered through it because she didn't want to ruin the walk. Anyway, by the time she realised she was bitterly cold and in real trouble, they were miles away from the house.

"I know, I'm sorry."

Emilia squeezed her shoulder tightly. "No need to apologise. I'm just glad you're okay now. Are you feeling warmer?"

"Much." Amber turned her face towards the flames. Because she'd been so cold for so long, she knew it would take a while for the warmth to circulate within her body. Sitting in front of the fire felt lovely. She relished the scorching heat on her cold face.

She leaned a little into Emilia's half-hug. It felt nice to be held, she couldn't remember the last time she had sat and just enjoyed a fire with someone.

"We will do something inside tomorrow, I promise." Emilia's hand softly rubbed up and down her arm.

The movement was hypnotic. Amber felt a different kind of heat building within her. Her last relationship had been months ago. Her recent stress at work was not exactly conducive to dating. She'd always been tactile, but she was only now realising how much she had missed the touch of another person.

Emilia smelt of simple, pure scents like vanilla. Nothing like the complex perfume that Amber wore.

Meanwhile, Emilia remained in her own world. "We can spend this time reading," Emilia said.

Suddenly the warmth of her body was missing, and Amber missed it instantly. She turned and watched as Emilia walked over to a bookshelf and started to pull out a few books.

"I can show you the original Lund collection," Emilia said. "Or some of the highlights, anyway."

She returned the sofa. Amber wished she would sit

thigh to thigh with her as she had done before, but she didn't. The gap between them was now filled with books. Emilia handled them as if they were made of fine china, opening them up and showing Amber the artwork.

Emilia was fully immersed in the beauty of the art within the books, excitedly showing Amber image after image. She explained the history behind them and shared stories her grandmother had told her of the origins of them all.

The drawings were nice enough, but Amber knew they wouldn't appeal to modern-day audiences. One of the first things publishing houses did to rejuvenate children's books was to create new imagery.

It was obvious that wasn't going to fly with Emilia. She was completely head over heels with the original books, including the art.

Amber considered that it was just another way that Emilia was stuck in time. She preferred the original every-thing. In some ways it was adorable, in others it was prob-lematic.

"How's your Swedish?" Emilia asked with a cheeky grin as she opened one of the books.

"Terrible," Amber replied.

"Would you like to learn some?"

I'd like you to sit closer, Amber thought. She knew it wasn't just the body heat that she missed, but she pushed that particular feeling down. Emilia was being so sweet and kind. She didn't need Amber being inappropriate and turning a kind gesture into something it wasn't.

"I'll try, but I warn you… it's not my strength," Amber said.

Emilia grabbed the books that were sandwiched between them and placed them on the coffee table. She shuffled up so she was right beside Amber, nudging the crocheted blanket so she was also underneath it.

"Well, I'm a great teacher." Emilia placed the book on their laps.

Amber inhaled her scent again. *Is it perfume, or just soap? Or her natural scent? Does anyone naturally smell of vanilla?*

"This was my mother's favourite book," Emilia continued, unaware of Amber's distraction.

"And now you're going to let me ruin it for you?" Amber chuckled.

"No! I have faith in you," Emilia promised. "Are you warm enough? Should I get you some hot chocolate before we start?"

Amber couldn't remember the last time someone wanted to look after her like that. Probably when she was a child. Hot chocolate, an open fire, and a warm blanket sounded amazing, but she had no interest in Emilia leaving her again.

She shook her head. "I'm good. Let's learn some Swedish."

18

AN ACCIDENTAL SIGHTING

EMILIA LOCKED the front door and then switched off the lights as she walked towards the stairs to go up to bed. It had been a wonderful evening, but she was still kicking herself for not realising that Amber had been having such a terrible time during the day.

She should have realised that someone not used to long walks in freezing temperatures would suffer. It hadn't even occurred to her that Amber wouldn't be used to the cold. Now she realised that Amber's one-word answers and complete silence were simply because she was too cold to speak.

"*Vad jag är dum*," she mumbled to herself.

She couldn't believe that she hadn't even taken the time to check with Amber that she would want to go on an hours-long walk out in the snow. She'd just assumed that she would because Emilia was such a fan of it. Also, because she wanted to show off her favourite place in the world to her new friend.

The cold and persistent wind, along with the wet snow

and the generally cold temperatures, had affected Amber greatly. The moment Emilia's fingers touched her cheek she had realised how badly. If it was just a usual chill, Amber would have warmed up following her shower and their eating dinner, but she hadn't and was cold to the touch.

Emilia had felt awful, as if she had broken her new friend. She felt like a child on Christmas morning who had received and subsequently wrecked her present.

She climbed the stairs, turning off the hallway light and stepping into the darkness of her bedroom. Directly opposite was the guesthouse bedroom. Unintentionally, she looked up and saw Amber pulling off her top as she prepared for bed.

Emilia fell to the floor in her haste to not be caught looking. Although, it was an accident. It wasn't her fault that Amber's light was on, that her bedroom was directly opposite, and that she'd walked in just at the moment she was exposing herself.

She crawled along the floor towards the window. Grabbing the edge of the curtain, she flicked her wrist to try to drag it closed. After a few unsuccessful attempts, she finally succeeded.

She let out a relieved breath and sat with her back to the radiator. Now she just had to hope that Amber hadn't seen her. Surely she hadn't? Emilia hadn't had the chance to turn a light on, so the room would have been dark.

She placed the back of her hand to her cheek, surprised to find it was hot. She assumed it was from the panic and from crawling across the floor.

Blinking a few times to clear the sight of Amber's bra

from her vision, she tried to think of what they could do the next day. Nothing came immediately to mind. Most of the things she enjoyed were outside in nature.

If she were to prove to Hugo that she was able to make friends—and not make them miserable and cold—she needed to think outside the box.

She got to her feet, checked the curtains were fully closed, and then turned on a light. Conversations with Amber raced through her mind as she tried to recall things she enjoyed.

Evidently, she'd made an error in assuming that Amber would appreciate all the things that she did. It seemed so obvious now: friendships were about give and take. And people were very different from each other. She needed to consider Amber's likes and dislikes.

Shopping, she thought.

Amber had mentioned more than once that she enjoyed going shopping with her friends. They would meet at a large shopping mall and stroll around for hours, eating lunch and chatting as they went.

Emilia shivered at the thought. She'd been to one of the city malls a couple of times when she really needed to buy something that she couldn't get from town. It was often crowded, overly bright, and very loud. All the things she hated most.

But she knew it would make Amber happy and would keep her warm. They couldn't very well snuggle up on the sofa in front of the fire every night, even if she had enjoyed it. It had probably been hellish for Amber considering how cold she'd been.

She made up her mind. They'd go to the mall. It wasn't

her thing, but friendship meant compromise and she wanted to prove to both Amber and Hugo that she could do that.

She hoped that she was making progress on that front. Thankfully, the dreaded topic of the contract had only been brought up a couple of times during the day. Both times she had managed to push the subject aside with relative ease.

As time went by, she knew she was making it harder and harder to admit that she had no intention of ever talking about business with Amber, but she comforted herself in the knowledge that, hopefully, Amber's goals were changing from business to friendship.

SHOPPING

THE TIMID KNOCK on the front door caused Amber to look up from her book. As much as she hated being offline, she had to admit that the unexpected free time meant she had torn through the paperback she had brought for the plane journey. Another evening and she'd have finished it.

Emilia stood on the porch outside, looking at her through the window in the door and giving her a wave.

Amber quickly walked over and let the woman in.

"Good morning," Emilia greeted.

"Hi, I didn't know if you were up yet," Amber admitted. "I was just getting some coffee and catching up on some reading. Can I get you a cup?"

"Yes, that would be nice. Thank you." Emilia removed her loosely tied scarf and hung it on one of the hooks by the door.

Amber pulled another cup from the shelf by the coffee machine and placed it by the empty one she had previously fetched for herself. She'd put the filter coffee on a while ago but had then got so caught up in her book that she had completely forgotten about it.

Suddenly, she remembered why she had forgotten about the coffee. The romantic element in her novel was coming to a rather intense conclusion. She spun around just as Emilia was picking up the book and looking at the back cover with interest.

"It's… for work," Amber said. She placed the coffee cups on the table.

"I thought you only worked with children's books?"

"I… do."

"This is a romance book. A lesbian romance book."

Amber's heart felt like it had stopped. Emilia was looking at her with an expression she couldn't read. Amber resisted the urge to snatch the book out of her hands and deny its existence.

"It's… for a colleague. At work."

Emilia turned the paperback over. "*This* is a Walker Clay book?"

Amber knew for a fact that it was a self-published book. She also knew that her lie was rapidly unravelling.

"Okay, it's not for work. It's a guilty pleasure." She laughed lightly, trying to defuse the situation.

"Are you a lesbian?" Emilia asked, her face still neutral, completely unreadable to Amber.

This is what you wanted, she reminded herself. *To be honest about your sexuality. Now's the time.*

"I'm bisexual," she confessed quietly.

"Is there much bisexual fiction?" Emilia looked at the book with interest.

"Not really. There's M/M and F/F. Many have bisexual

characters but not a lot on the bisexual category itself…" She trailed off. She was about to go into far too much explanation of her guilty-pleasure reading habits.

"That makes sense." Emilia put the book down and picked up the coffee cup. "So, I was thinking today we could go to the shopping mall, if that is something you would like? It will be inside and warm, and you can see some of our shops. We can eat out, which you're a fan of." She winked cheekily.

Amber's head was spinning. Emilia seemingly had nothing to say about her bisexuality or her choice in reading matter. Which was, of course, wonderful. But it left her wondering what Emilia's thoughts on the subject were.

Not that she was about to quiz her, but she did need to know more.

"You're okay with me being…"

Emilia looked endearingly perplexed. "Being?"

"Bisexual."

"Of course, why wouldn't I be?" Emilia asked. She put the book down on the table and pointed to the cup of coffee still sat on the kitchen counter. "Is that for me?"

"Um. Yes, yes…" She turned and picked up the mug, handing it over. "Sorry."

"Thank you. So, do you want to go shopping?"

Amber was still trying to process how someone with such old-fashioned views in some ways could also not bat an eyelash at the news she was bisexual. She wondered if she was misreading Emilia, if she was bothered by the fact but was keeping a lid on her emotions. But that wasn't really like her at all.

Emilia seemed to wear her heart on her sleeve. Maybe she was honestly not concerned about Amber's sexuality.

"Amber?" Emilia asked, drawing her attention again. "Do you want to go shopping?"

Amber shook the cobwebs from her mind.

"Yes… that sounds great." She narrowed her eyes. "But you don't seem to be much of a shopping person?"

Emilia shrugged. "I like shopping."

Amber didn't believe her for one moment, but she appreciated the gesture. And she wasn't about to look the gift horse of indoor warmth in the mouth.

"Great. That sounds like fun." Amber was already salivating at the prospect of having some connectivity on her phone. She could check her messages and download some entertainment to keep her going for the next few days. She already knew that her paperback wasn't about to last her much longer, grabbing a few ebooks from the cloud would be essential.

"Good. I'll call a taxi to take us there," Emilia said.

Amber pointed out of the window towards the hire car. "Or I can drive us?"

"I…" Emilia trailed off as she looked out at the car. "Yes, okay."

It was obvious that something was wrong, but Amber couldn't figure out what. Before she had a chance to say anything else, Emilia was on her feet.

"I'll leave you to get ready. Shall we leave in around thirty minutes?"

"Whenever you're ready; I'm just reading," Amber admitted.

Emilia smiled and picked up the book again. "I like romance stories; do you recommend this one?"

Amber's face heated at the racy sex scene she'd just read. Twice.

"It's… good," she said half-heartedly. She wasn't sure if it was something Emilia would be interested in. She couldn't picture Emilia reading raunchy books, but then again, she didn't know her well enough to say that. For all she knew, Emilia might have an entire bookcase dedicated to erotica, but Amber would bet heavily that Emilia didn't read lesbian romance.

"Maybe I will borrow it from you?" Emilia asked.

Maybe I'm wrong, Amber thought. She slowly nodded her head, not knowing what else to say.

Amber pulled the car into the parking space and yanked up the handbrake. She averted her eyes as Emilia peeled her fingers away from the seat. As she had pretended to not notice that she'd maintained that particular death grip for the entire journey.

Emilia was obviously not a fan of being a passenger. No wonder she walked or cycled everywhere. She wondered if Emilia usually put her faith in a specific taxi driver, one with whom she felt comfortable.

Amber placed her bag in her lap. She flipped down the visor and started to reapply her lipstick. It didn't need to be done, but she suspected that Emilia needed a few moments to compose herself.

She was by no means a fast driver. In fact, she had

driven deliberately slowly and carefully the entire way. That hadn't prevented Emilia's rapid, shallow breathing and tight grasp on the leather seat.

Amber didn't know if the fear was caused by being out, being in a car, or the prospect of going into a busy shopping centre.

Or possibly all three.

She decided to keep a close eye on Emilia to be sure she wasn't sacrificing too much in order to appease her. It was strange how the tables had turned—just the day before she was happily ignoring her own wishes to keep Emilia happy. Now Emilia was doing the same for her. The difference being that Amber had simply felt cold and miserable, while Emilia's usual healthy complexion had gone decidedly pale.

"Is there anything specific you want to look for?" she asked casually.

"Um. No… I… just looking around is fine." Emilia looked around the brightly lit underground car park as if she were in a rough neighbourhood.

"Great, we'll keep it nice and light and simple then. Just a stroll around and see what we see."

They exited the car and walked through the large car park towards the central escalators that took them up into the middle of the mall.

Amber was used to large shopping centres from London and expected something much smaller. To her surprise, the mall was enormous. Three levels spread as far as she could see in all directions. The building had modern Swedish architectural style, with lots of light colours and glass.

Just like any other city mall close to the Christmas season, it was packed with people. As the escalator carried them to the next level of the centre, Amber turned around to get a subtle look at her companion.

Emilia's eyes darted around, and she worried her lip. It was painfully obvious that she was skirting close to a possible panic attack.

"I think we should stop in a nice, quiet coffee shop first," Amber suggested.

Emilia nodded. Amber wasn't sure she'd even heard her or registered what she'd said.

She looked around and saw the perfect establishment. It had comfortable chairs and was large enough that it could swallow a lot of people and not feel crowded. As they reached the top of the escalator, she took Emilia's arm and guided her towards the coffee shop. She could feel how tense Emilia was through her thick jacket and the sweater.

Once inside, she led the way towards the back of the shop and gestured for Emilia to sit down in a soft tub chair. She took off her scarf and jacket and looked over to the counter.

"What can I get you? Tea? Do you want some food?"

Emilia's glazed eyes looked at the counter and then up at the menu.

Amber's heart panged with guilt. Emilia was so far out of her comfort zone that she was having difficulty operating. She couldn't believe the sacrifice Emilia had made in order for them to do something Amber enjoyed. As much as she hated the cold from the previous day, she knew it paled in comparison to how Emilia was coping with the stress of a busy mall.

Emilia agreed to the idea of tea, and Amber hurried off to get it. As she queued, she kept an eye on Emilia at the back of the café. As time went by and she slowly got closer to being served, she was relieved to see Emilia appear to calm down. Her eyes no longer raced along the crowds outside the shop, and she relaxed her posture a little.

Amber bought a couple of traditional Swedish cakes—one foul-coloured green thing and one innocent-looking pastry. She suspected that Emilia would feel a little better after some sugar. Plus, while Emilia got herself together, Amber could take some time to look at her phone, to see how much the world had changed in the last couple of days. It felt like it had been a month.

She grabbed one of the free papers on her return and set everything up on the table.

"Cakes?" Emilia asked. She looked happy at their appearance.

"Soaking up the culture," Amber said.

Emilia explained what both of the cakes were called, and Amber decided she'd continue to call them the green thing and the pastry thing.

She was beyond pleased to see that Emilia looked much improved and was communicating again. She decided to give them both some more time before hitting the shops.

"I'm sorry to be rude, but I really need to check my emails," Amber said as she got her phone out of her pocket and put it on the table. She handed Emilia the paper. "Do you mind if we sit and hang out here for a while?"

As she'd expected, a look of relief washed over Emilia's face.

"Of course, if you need to work, then we will stay here as long as you need." Emilia happily started reading the paper.

Amber wasn't about to explain that emails weren't just for work. She was just happy that Emilia had recuperated and that she had some time to be on her phone.

20

SPIRALLING

EMILIA WALKED around the bookstore with a stack of books piled high in her hands. She wasn't entirely comfortable being at the busy mall, but frequent stops in quieter shops were making her feel better.

She suspected that Amber hadn't really wanted to go into the bookstore. After all, why would she? All of the books were in a foreign language. It must have been like going into a candy shop after visiting the dentist to have your mouth wired closed.

And yet Amber had insisted, right around the time that Emilia was finding the clothing shop they were in a little overwhelming. Like she somehow knew. Emilia hoped she wasn't that transparent. She wanted Amber to have a good time and not worry about her too much.

But she had to confess that she was loving the bookshop.

She looked up and saw Amber strolling around, picking up books and looking at their covers momentarily before putting them down again. She was obviously giving Emilia time and space to collect herself and feel better.

It was working. She felt safe surrounded by books, many of which she hadn't read before. Her local bookstore was small. The newsletter of new releases was sufficient, but nothing was like walking around a large shop. She'd quickly stacked six books up in her hands and considered them necessary purchases. A couple more followed after a few minutes.

The rumbling cacophony of the hordes of shoppers sat just outside the doors. She tried to tune it out, to no avail. She'd known it would be busy and horrible at the mall, but nothing could have prepared her for how bad it was.

During the car journey she had felt near to a panic attack. With every passing mile that she travelled, her breathing had become more laboured. She pulled herself together as best she could for Amber's sake. She had promised that they would have a nice day shopping in the warmth, and that was exactly what she intended to do. Anxiety be damned.

A book was added to the pile in her hands.

"I think you'll like this one," Amber said. "It's got a lot of twists and turns, I won't spoil it."

"Thank you." She peered at the top of the stack, interested to see what Amber would suggest for her. It looked like a cosy mystery book, something she enjoyed immensely. Especially when they contained recipes.

"Would you like some help carrying those?" Amber asked.

Emilia looked at the books on the tables and then the

books in her hands. She had many more tables to visit before she was done. She would certainly run out of space in her arms before then.

"Yes, please."

Amber took the majority of the pile from her.

"I'm sorry, this must be very boring for you," she apologised.

"Not at all. I like looking at all the translations and seeing what changed regarding the covers. Or when things stayed exactly the same. I'm sure that sounds strange to you."

"Not at all. Many of the books I read are released in English first, so it's interesting to see what happens if it goes on to be translated."

"Great, I'll leave you to it. I'm going to see what's hot in YA," Amber said as she departed with a smile.

Emilia wasn't sure that Amber was as interested as she claimed, but she appreciated the sentiment. A while longer in the security of the soft furnishings and jazz playlist and she'd hopefully be feeling rejuvenated and ready to move on to the next store.

A loud noise outside caused her to jump. She looked around and noticed it was a group of teenagers dressed up in Christmas hats, shouting and laughing. She took a few deep breaths. She hoped that the shopping visit would soon be declared a success by Amber and that they could leave.

She just needed to keep it together a while longer.

Lunch was frantic. Everyone in the mall had decided to eat around the same time, and every single eatery was packed with people. In the end, Amber had sat Emilia at a table in the only café with space and gone to queue.

Emilia gripped her scarf in her hands, watching as people with trays milled around the restaurant looking for a spare table. She hated being at an empty table. She wondered if people thought she was rude for sitting there. Or worse, if someone was going to ask to sit with her. It wasn't a very Swedish thing to do, but external influences were changing people's perceptions. Or maybe a tourist would come and sit with her. Maybe someone chatty.

She shivered.

She looked at the queue and willed it to move quicker. She wanted Amber with her. The whole day had been rescued by Amber knowing what she needed and providing it for her. Somehow Amber could detect when she was starting to lose control and quickly swooped in and made everything better, without even saying anything.

Real panic was starting to seep in. Emilia was finding it difficult to get enough breath, and her lungs felt sore from the effort and lack of oxygen. She let go of her scarf and gripped the table, needing something more solid to hold on to.

Oh no, not now.

It had been years since she'd had a full-blown panic attack. Not that she could remember it. She'd been out with Hugo, and the next thing she knew, she was at home. She'd passed out cold, her body just shut down to save her from herself.

She was spiralling. Just the *thought* of having a panic

attack made her anxiety ratchet up several notches, which she knew brought the whole likelihood of passing out that much closer.

Her vision was starting to lose focus, and black started to creep in around the edges. She slammed her eyes closed and held on to the table. She wondered if she'd flop onto the table or knock the whole thing over when she did finally collapse.

"Hey." The voice sounded familiar but so distant.

She felt arms wrap around her, keeping her upright.

"Emilia, can you open your eyes for me?"

It was only then that she realised her eyes were tightly scrunched closed. She focused as hard as she could on the simple task of opening her eyes. After a few long moments, she managed to open them just enough to let a little of the bright light in.

She winced. She could feel her brow was furrowed, causing a headache to start.

"I think we should go home."

Emilia looked at the woman sitting beside her, arms still wrapped solidly around her.

Amber, she remembered. *Home*. She felt relieved at the thought.

"Do you think you're okay to walk?"

Emilia didn't know.

She noticed a man approaching her. Suddenly Amber was in a conversation with him, but she couldn't make out any of the words. She burrowed her face in the tall collar of her jacket, hoping to shy away from the attention she must have been drawing to herself.

She wanted to be home. She wished she had never left.

She started to gasp for breath. Everything was fading in and out and suddenly… it was black.

PIZZA FIXES EVERYTHING

AMBER DROVE SLOWLY BACK to Emilia's farmhouse on the edge of the city. Every now and then she glanced over at the sleeping woman beside her to make sure she was okay.

She'd left the queue at the café when she noticed that Emilia had gone deathly pale and was looking faint. It was only a few minutes later when the inevitable had happened and Emilia blacked out in her arms.

Luckily a doctor happened to be shopping at the time and rushed to the rescue. While Amber was talking with him, Emilia had slackened. She was heavier than she looked, and Amber was grateful that the doctor helped her to save Emilia from hitting the floor.

Emilia came around quickly but was still out of it. The doctor had quickly agreed with Amber's diagnosis of exhaustion and generally being overwhelmed. He'd kindly helped Amber walk Emilia to the car and even left his business card in case she needed to contact him later.

As soon as they were in the car, Emilia had fallen asleep.

Amber couldn't blame her, she must have been exhausted. If she were honest with herself, she was drained as well.

The moment she realised that Emilia was going to pass out—and had thankfully caught her slim body in an awkward bearhug—she realised something. Emilia meant *something* to her.

She meant more than the contract which had impossibly slipped her mind on more than one occasion. At some point it had morphed from a business relationship to a friendship… and maybe even more. Seeing Emilia struggle with her fears had been difficult and Amber had wanted to sweep her into a hug and protect her from the modern world which she obviously found so disturbing.

She'd been around people with anxiety before, but nothing as serious as the symptoms Emilia was exhibiting. She was still uncertain what the root cause of the anxiety was, and knew she was not qualified to diagnose it herself. Whatever it was, it was clearly a lot more debilitating than Amber had first realised.

She wondered if Emilia had always suffered with crippling anxiety, if that was the reason for her reclusive lifestyle. Or had refusing to leave the house made the anxiety worse? Without knowing more about Emilia and her history, it was impossible to say.

She felt to blame. Without her presence, Emilia would never have found herself in the shopping mall. She would have been happily walking around her beloved lake and identifying distant birdcalls.

Emilia let out a groan. Amber indicated and quickly pulled the car over to the side of the road.

"Hey, welcome back." She turned to regard Emilia, sitting back to give her some room as her eyes flickered opened.

Emilia looked around the car in confusion, her eyes wild and unfocused.

"*Var är jag?*"

Amber had never felt so useless in all her life. Emilia was scared and in need of comfort, and the only Swedish phrase she had managed to learn was *God Jul*. Wishing her a Merry Christmas now wasn't going to help.

She ignored the language switch and hoped that Emilia would be able to cope with speaking English. "How are you feeling?"

Emilia looked at her, her eyes slowly becoming less wild. Realisation seemed to set in. She looked around the car, and a deep blush started up her throat and onto her cheeks.

"Did I faint?"

"You did," Amber confirmed. She handed over a bottle of water. "Have a drink."

Emilia grasped the bottle in both hands and took a small sip. "I'm so sorry."

"There's nothing to be sorry for."

"I must have made a terrible scene."

"Not really. Everyone was too busy Christmas shopping to care about what you were doing. And a really hunky doctor literally leapt to our rescue. He vaulted over a bench, it was great."

Emilia started to smile. "You're just being kind."

"No, seriously, he was buff. He must live in the gym.

He offered to carry you but then you woke up and were able to walk so, you know, bad timing on your part."

Emilia started to laugh. "I don't remember."

"Never mind," Amber reassured her. She wasn't surprised Emilia couldn't remember. She'd been in a complete daze as she leant into Amber and allowed herself to be led to the car.

Emilia looked around. "We're going home?"

"We are. I got the hunky doctor to carry your books and my bags and now we're heading home. Satnav says we're about twenty minutes away." She pointed to the screen.

"I am sorry," Emilia repeated.

"Seriously, there's no need to be sorry. But you and I do need to start learning to communicate. I promise to tell you when I'm freezing to death if you promise to tell me when you're feeling overwhelmed. I know crowds can be a bit much. You don't need to try to be a hero."

She looked at her seriously, wishing Emilia would understand that she wasn't in any way angry or disappointed. In fact, she was concerned. Emilia had quickly become very important to her and seeing her suffer had been difficult to say the least.

Amber was fighting the instinct to wrap her arms around Emilia and hold her close and tell her that everything would be okay.

"I feel very silly," Emilia confessed, refusing to make eye contact as she studied the dashboard.

Amber's heart broke. Emilia was so sweet and open with her feelings. She didn't know if it was a fundamental part of her persona, or the fact that she had grown up in such a small and insular world that she had never learnt any different. Whatever the reason, it was adorable.

She'd struggled to admit when she wasn't feeling well, but that was solely for Amber's benefit. Putting Amber's wishes above her own health. That aside, Emilia was often an open book.

"You don't need to feel silly. You couldn't control it. And truth be told, I could tell you were suffering a little beforehand and I didn't do enough to make sure that you were okay. So, technically, I'm silly."

"You're not sill—"

Amber held up her hand. "No, I refuse to have a debate with you about who is the silliest. Not until you have shown me where that local pizzeria is."

"Pizza?"

"Well, we both know that I can't cook, but I can buy dinner. And I think you need a nice, big, greasy pizza to make you feel better. We can take it home and eat it on a plate like a grown-up. Best of both worlds."

Emilia seemed to agree with that, slowly nodding her head. She still looked so young and lost. Amber promised herself that she would dote on Emilia that evening. If she didn't, who would?

A QUIET EVENING IN

"Should we?" Emilia asked. She bit her lip and looked down at the pizza box in her hand and then up at the fireplace.

"It's your house, you can do whatever you like," Amber said.

Emilia technically knew that was true, but she'd never eaten dinner in front of the fire before. She'd never eaten dinner from a box rather than a plate. It was like breaking multiple unwritten rules all at once.

The very thought of sitting at the brightly lit dining table and having to get out plates and cutlery was just too much. When Amber had casually suggested eating in front of the fire, it was like Emilia's world had been tilted. Again. But this time it was a good tilt, this time it was in the name of comfort. And what she really needed right now was comfort.

"Okay!" she decided. She handed her pizza box to Amber. "I'll be right back. Please, start eating."

She rushed away, eager to get out of her clothes and

into something more comfortable. In particular, she wanted to get into her comfortable woollen socks that her grandmother had made for her mother years ago. They were a slice of home that always made her feel better no matter what the day had brought her.

It only took her a couple of minutes to throw her clothes on the bedroom floor and dress herself in comfortable jeans, a baggy sweater, and her favourite woollen socks. She bounded down the stairs again and into the living room.

Amber had pushed the coffee table to one side and was sitting on the rug with two pizza boxes and two cans of soda beside her. Emilia quickly joined her, pulling a thin blanket over her shoulders, more for comfort than to keep out any chill.

"Nice socks," Amber said with a smirk.

"They were my mother's," Emilia replied. "Made by my grandmother."

"I can tell." Amber laughed and passed her pizza box over to her.

"There's nothing wrong with these socks," Emilia defended through a smile.

"Whatever you say. They just appear to be a little more hole than sock."

"They are just perfect, thank you very much." Emilia took a large bite of pizza while smiling at Amber.

It felt good to eat. And so good to be home. She still felt shaken up by everything that had happened, but she knew she was now fully on the road to recovery.

That said, the whole drama had made her consider that maybe she wasn't supposed to have friends. Things had been going so well with Amber, but then she had ruined it by being… her.

What kind of person can't even go to a mall? she asked herself. *And who faints in public just because it's too busy and noisy?*

Her pulse started to race again. She took a deep breath before eating another bite of pizza. She stared at the flames flickering in the fireplace. Being home felt good, but it also felt like a failure. Like she'd had to retreat. Yes, home was safe, but that didn't mean she had to like it right now.

"You're angry-thinking," Amber whispered.

"I'm not," Emilia denied.

"You are. Your face is all scrunched up. And you're rage-eating."

"Angry-thinking and rage-eating are not things."

"They are, you're doing them both." Amber playfully elbowed her.

She stopped eating and lowered the slice of pizza into the box. "Fine. I'm angry at myself."

"I know. It will die down," Amber reassured her.

"You're not going to tell me to not worry?"

"Would you listen?"

Emilia considered that for a few seconds. "No. I'd carry on being angry."

"There you go then. You're angry, it will die down." Amber opened up a can of soda and took a long sip straight from the can.

Emilia wondered how Amber could know her so well after so little time together. It seemed amazing that Amber knew exactly what to do and what to say, while she was ruining everything.

A new theory asserted itself in her mind. Maybe Amber was capable of making friends with Emilia, but Emilia was incapable of returning the favour.

Could there be a possibility that her isolation and solitary ways weren't the reasons for her lack of friends? Maybe she was just no good at it.

Suddenly, she felt a desperate longing to see Hugo. Her closest friend, the one who understood everything about her. Dear, sweet Hugo, who was always there for her and never wavered. She never pushed him away with her foolish behaviour.

She decided to use the phone he had given her to text him and invite him to dinner. Then she could prove to Hugo that she could make new friends. And prove to Amber that she had a friend, because surely Amber must have had her doubts by now?

He would also be able to help on the conversation front, which she was clearly lacking on. When Amber was quiet, they were both quiet.

The whole idea of her being able to make friends now seemed utterly ridiculous. She couldn't believe that she had thought she could do it.

"So, tell me about these winter markets?" Amber asked.

Emilia blinked a couple of times. She realised that she had become lost in her own thoughts. She was so consumed with assuming that she was unable to make conversation that she had remained silent until Amber took up the mantle.

"They are wooden buildings, selling different things. Food… gifts." She paused. "It's outside, though, so it will be cold."

She didn't want Amber to freeze like she had the day before, even if she did want to show her the markets. It was one of the few shopping experiences she actually enjoyed, being outside in the fresh air and having the option to walk to the side and leave the crowds at any point. And she only attended in the middle of the day, in the middle of the week, when she knew it would be quiet.

"I'll remember to wrap up warm," Amber said.

Emilia knew it was an olive branch, and she was grateful for it.

"You can borrow some scarves, I have lots of them. They were knitted by my grandmother and my mother."

"Ah, full of holes then?" Amber joked.

"No," Emilia lightly admonished her. "They will keep you nice and warm. But if you get cold, then you must tell me immediately and we will go home."

"Agreed. And if you feel in the slightest bit over-whelmed, you must tell me."

Emilia nodded her agreement.

Amber nodded towards the bookcase. "Will you read with me again tonight? I felt like I was getting the hang of this Swedish business last night."

Emilia chuckled. Amber's pronunciation was terrible, but her accent was adorable. Emilia would never admit to making Amber repeat the same few words over and over again because it sounded so cute.

"Sure, maybe you can read a whole one to me?" Emilia suggested.

"Haven't you suffered enough?" Amber laughed.

"Reading with you isn't punishment," Emilia said seriously. "I enjoy it a lot."

"Me too," Amber admitted in a soft whisper.

The atmosphere in the room had changed. Emilia didn't know when or why, but she knew it had. And she didn't dislike it.

23

HOW DIFFERENT WE ARE

EMILIA SNUGGLED into Amber's side and watched as she flipped through photographs on her phone, showing Emilia more of her day-to-day life.

They'd started off reading, but Amber soon became disheartened with the extra letters and the strange grammar rules that applied to Swedish. Emilia found she couldn't explain why things were the way they were, she just knew what was right and what wasn't.

After a short debate about grammar, and how some things just didn't make sense, they'd put the books to one side. They leaned against each other and chatted in soft tones. Amber talked about her family, her childhood, her schooling, and university. She'd slid her phone out of her pocket and started to scroll through photographs of friends, holidays, family birthdays, and more.

Emilia soaked it all up. She couldn't believe how much Amber did. One day she was skiing on a dry ski slope with her friends from an old job, the next day she was at an aquarium with someone she met at a bar.

Amber was adventurous and outgoing. Emilia was still in awe from having eaten pizza in the living room directly from the box. She wondered why she had never done it before. It was such a simple pleasure and one she could recreate easily, but it had never even occurred to her.

"Oh, ignore that one," Amber said, swiping past a picture of a drunken night out.

Emilia's cheeks heated up at the split-second sight of Amber in an intense lip lock with another woman.

"Your girlfriend?" Emilia asked. She knew she should leave the subject alone, but she was suddenly desperate to know. Amber had claimed she was single, but that was before she admitted she was bisexual. She wondered if that was a lie and Amber hadn't wanted to out herself at first.

"Ex. I'm single, have been for way too long," Amber confessed. "Work gets in the way."

Emilia decided to remain silent. She'd been single for ages, and work had nothing to do with it. She wondered if Amber assumed that she was a never-been-kissed hermit. Suddenly she felt the need to let Amber know that simply wasn't the case.

"Yes, it's been a while since my last relationship, too," she said.

Amber was still scrolling through photos of the night out, and Emilia wondered if she'd even heard her. She couldn't repeat herself, even if she did so desperately want Amber to know that she'd not always been single.

"I envy you," she admitted as Amber hurriedly scrolled through various pictures of parties.

"Why?"

"Because you have so many friends and you are always

doing things with them," Emilia explained. "Not that I'd want that, I'd need to be a different person to be able to cope with it. But it seems nice in theory."

"I envy you," Amber said, not looking up as she scrolled through endless dark pictures. "Sometimes, I just want to be at home. But then home is a cold and lonely place, so I end up going out. You've made your house your safe place, and it's beautiful and homely and I can understand why you love it so much."

Emilia didn't know what to say. She didn't think anyone could ever envy her life. Especially not someone as impressive as Amber.

Maybe the grass is always greener, she considered.

The party pictures ended, and there was a picture of Amber sitting on a small chair with a child on her lap, reading a book.

"Who's that?" Emilia asked.

"That's Michael. I'm a part of a local reading group. I donate books from work, and sometimes I read them to the kids. He's dyslexic so reading is tough, but he's getting better all the time."

"It's nice that you take the time to do that."

"It's important," Amber said. "I used to read so much as a child. My mum would joke that I read the print off so many of our books. I think reading is so important, it's why I went into the career I did. Without reading, you can't learn or grow."

Emilia knew they were skating dangerously close to the subject that she had been trying to avoid, business and the dreaded contract that she had no intention of signing.

"Oh! Remember to wear two pairs of socks to the

market tomorrow," she changed the subject in a way she hoped was tactful. "In case your feet start to get cold."

"I'll be fine," Amber promised. "Besides, I don't think you'll be able to get me out from under this blanket."

She nestled deeper into the material, and Emilia felt every point where their bodies touched. It was a bizarre feeling, she'd cuddled under blankets with Hugo in the past, but she'd never felt like this. With Hugo things felt comfortable, warm, and friendly. This felt like more.

She knew it was probably wrong and something she should put a stop to, but she didn't want to. And there was no way she was going to admit her feelings to Amber, in case she pulled away and the moment ended.

"Now, this picture has a story behind her," Amber started as she scrolled to the next image in her library.

Emilia burrowed in closer, under the guise that she was leaning in to look at the photo. She only half-listened to Amber's softly spoken story. Instead she focused on the feel of Amber's warm body beside her, the vibration of her voice, the scent of her perfume.

Her day had been a horrible and traumatic experience, but her evening was turning out to be more perfect than she could ever imagine.

In the back of her mind, she knew that all that would have to end soon.

24

CHRISTMAS MARKET

AMBER FELT as if she had fallen into a typical stock photo of a charming Christmas market. She'd often thought about going to visit a winter market in Europe, but the timing was never right.

She held onto Emilia's arm as they strolled past the wooden huts with various products for sale. Strings of lights ran in a zigzag from building to building, and in the middle of everything was a tall Christmas tree decorated in simple, elegant white lights.

The weather was dark and gloomy. Occasionally snow fell in light dustings, but it only added to the atmosphere.

"This place is perfect," Amber said for about the tenth time since they arrived.

"Do you not have Christmas markets back home?"

"We do in some places, but they are nothing like this. This is… classy."

Emilia chuckled. "You are silly."

It was her go-to descriptor for Amber, said with a light and kind tone. She suspected Emilia was actually so surprised that anything could be different to what she knew that it was automatically labelled as silly.

She tightened her grip on Emilia's arm and whispered in her ear, "Never change."

Emilia looked at her curiously but didn't say anything.

They continued walking for a while, the smells of various foods and drinks mixing into a perfect Christmas blend. She could smell meats cooking and sweet treats flavoured with nutmeg and cinnamon.

"You have to try *glögg*," Emilia said, pointing towards a stall.

"Isn't that mulled wine?"

"Sort of." Emilia scrunched her nose up, clearly not quite happy with the comparison. "We add raisins and almonds to the bottom of the glass. And it's much more alcoholic."

"Oh, I see," she teased. "You're trying to get me drunk."

"No!" Emilia's cheeks became even redder than the cold air had already made them. "Never, I—"

"I'm just joking," Amber reassured her. "I can't try any. I'm driving, remember?"

"Oh, yes, sorry. When I come here with Hugo we always take a taxi. I forgot."

Amber sighed. She was almost becoming fed up with the mention of Hugo. She was sure he was a very nice man, but it was painfully clear that he was Emilia's one and only friend. Everything was about Hugo.

Not that it was his fault. Or, in fact, anyone's fault. It just made Amber feel depressed that someone as wonderful as Emilia wasn't surrounded by friends.

"No problem, I'll take your word for it that it's delicious. I'll definitely try some of those buns, though."

She waited for Emilia to correct her and provide the name of the baked goods. When the silence continued, she looked at Emilia who appeared pensive.

"What's wrong?" Amber wondered if Emilia was starting to feel overwhelmed. She started to mentally plan a quiet route back to where she had parked the car.

"I… I lied to you," Emilia admitted.

Amber couldn't help but smile at the guilty expression. "Okay?"

"I *do* have a phone. Well, I didn't have one when you first contacted me. Well, I did but it was under my bed, dead. So, really, I didn't. But I would never have spoken to you on it, phones scare me a lot."

Amber tried to smother her grin. Emilia really was cute when she worked herself up like this.

"So, you have a phone?"

"Yes. I… I was thinking that I could text Hugo and ask him to come to dinner tonight, if he is free. We could eat some traditional food and have glögg, homemade, of course."

"That sounds like a great idea if he is available."

"I'm sure he will be. He doesn't like to miss out on my cooking," Emilia boasted.

"I can see why, you're an excellent cook," Amber said. "Does this mean we can buy some ingredients and stuff while we're here?" She looked around at the stalls, her mouth salivating at the prospect of buying some produce and trying it that evening.

"So, you're not mad?" Emilia asked as she dug around in her handbag.

"About what?"

"The phone."

"Oh, that! No. As you said, you wouldn't have spoken to me on it anyway, so what difference does it make?"

Emilia pulled out the most basic phone Amber had seen in years. It looked like something she would have given to her grandmother if she were still alive. She held back the snort of laughter that had risen up within her.

"I feel bad for making you come all the way here," Emilia confessed.

"Don't. I'm glad I came. We're getting to know each other, and I'm having a great time. We do need to talk about that contract at some point, though, before we have too much fun and all the time runs out."

Emilia paused, staring at the phone.

Amber chuckled. "Do you want some help with that? Do you even know how to text?"

"Do you know how to text in Swedish?" Emilia batted back, quick as a flash.

Amber laughed. "Touché!"

Emilia quickly typed out a text message, proving that her lack of physical technology wasn't due to a lack of technical ability.

"So, what kind of food should we get?" Amber asked.

"Whatever they have. We should have a true Swedish smorgasbord, or, in this case, a *Julbord*."

"Christmas table?" Amber translated, insanely pleased with herself in spite of the relatively simple translation.

"*Precis!*" Emilia looked genuinely proud of her. She

pulled her arm and dragged her towards one of the nearest food stands.

In what came as a shock to Amber, Emilia started engaging in a quick-fire conversation with the stall holder. Amber just watched as they chatted and laughed, with no idea what was being said.

She didn't mind being left out of the conversation because it was such a joy to see Emilia so happily engaging with someone. It was as if all of her nerves surrounding social interaction had been suspended while she planned her feast.

Amber decided to leave them to it and walked to a nearby stall. The owner smiled warmly at her but said nothing. She got the distinct impression that the man knew she was British, or at least *not* Swedish. She'd noticed this before, especially at the mall. Before she even opened her mouth to speak, she was being greeted in English rather than Swedish. She wondered what was giving her away.

"We'll need to stop by the supermarket on the way home."

Amber jumped at Emilia's sudden reappearance.

"Oops, sorry."

"It's okay, just didn't see you there." She looked down and was surprised to see Emilia already had two bags. "Wow, you don't hang around, do you?"

"No, I'm excited. I can't wait to share a traditional Christmas meal with you and Hugo. I don't often do things like this."

Amber was almost afraid to ask, but she did. "What do you normally do on Christmas Day?"

"Eve."

"Sorry?"

"Christmas Eve, we celebrate all the things you celebrate on Christmas Day on Christmas Eve, the twenty-fourth."

"Oh, wow. So, what do you do on the twenty-fifth?"

Emilia shrugged. "Nothing much. Oh, we'll need raisins for the glögg. I can get that here."

Amber watched her hurry off to another stall. She realised she never got an answer to what Emilia did over Christmas. She suspected she already knew. Nothing. Or hanging out with Hugo.

Meanwhile, she had so many invites to do things at Christmas that she always ended up feeling guilty towards those she didn't get time to see. As much as she enjoyed the holidays, they could be stressful and expensive. They often involved seeing around five to six different groups of people, at least three meals of some kind, and far too much drink.

The only good part about not being in communication with the outside world was that she knew friends and family were currently sending her texts inviting her to various events. Not receiving them meant that she might have a moment to herself over the festive period this year.

Most of the people she saw, she only saw once a year. Obligatory socialising. The worst kind.

A happy medium between her style of Christmas and Emilia's would have been perfect for Amber. A few friends, one location, nice and quiet. No constantly looking at her watch and rushing to the next venue. No hauling bags and bags of gifts to be given and to carry home at the end of the day. The gifts she received were usually socks and toiletries from well-meaning friends who had panic-bought multiple identical items to distribute to all the women they would see over the holidays. She often noticed that her friends had exactly the same scent through to March.

She found that she was looking forward to this new style of Christmas with Emilia. In fact, she had to admit that she really enjoyed Emilia's company. She was like a breath of fresh air, not at all what Amber had expected to feel. When she left London, she thought she had Emilia all figured out. To her mind, she was boring, predictable, and even to be pitied in some ways.

Amber's life was full of social events. If she wanted to, she could attend a new party every night. Emilia never left the house. At first glance, Amber had shaken her head and thought Emilia's life was something to be avoided.

But after a couple of days within the Emilia Lund bubble, she had a different perspective. It was calm and cosy in the Lund house. Evenings were warm and thoughtful. Cuddling up on the sofa with Emilia and just talking about life had been a revelation. She had laughed, reminisced, and engaged in deeper conversation over the last couple of days than she had in the last few months.

Just because she socialised a lot didn't mean she was actually discussing anything worthwhile. After a while, questions and answers became formulaic.

How was work?
Good, thanks. You?
Did you see that new drama last night?
Isn't the weather miserable?

Everything became the same. She spoke all the time without saying a word. Maybe it was because Emilia didn't have anything boring to draw on that the conversations were so rich and invigorating.

There was no discussing television shows. No talking about the weather. No answering the same mindless questions time and time again.

Instead there were thought-provoking discussions about a world of things. While Emilia's body rarely left the house, her mind was widely travelled due to her books.

Amber had to admit that snuggling up to the attractive woman played a large part in her enjoyment of those evenings. She assumed it was a Swedish thing to get under blankets in the winter months and sit closely together while whispering into the fire-lit room.

Emilia may have been unaffected by the closeness, but Amber certainly wasn't. Of course, she didn't say anything because she didn't want to upset the balance, or worse, offend Emilia.

Snow started to fall again. She took a deep breath and sucked in the crisp air. She would have to leave this magical wonderland soon. Go back to work and normal life. It wasn't something she was looking forward to at all. The next year would bring a new job, new challenges, and more of the same in the way of hectic nightlife.

She had to talk to Emilia about the contract soon. The idea of sullying their wonderful time with talk of business wasn't appealing, but she was there for a reason.

Obviously, she had gained Emilia's trust. The woman had said she only did business with people she knew on a personal level. It was true that they knew each other well.

In a short space of time, they had become friends, and despite Amber's desperate attempts to push her feelings down, she knew that if the circumstances were different she would have happily been more than friends with Emilia.

She turned and sought out Emilia, quickly finding her chatting with another stallholder. Snowflakes were sticking to her woollen hat. She looked adorable. Amber had to stop herself from going to her and sweeping her into a warm hug.

Just keep it together for another couple of days, Amber told herself. *You can make it through.*

HUGO'S MISTAKE

AMBER HAD REPEATEDLY OFFERED to help prepare dinner, only for Emilia to repeatedly tell her that she was a guest and should relax instead. She couldn't sit and watch Emilia working so hard, so she decided to shower and freshen up before meeting Hugo.

He had returned Emilia's text message with a large number of random upper and lowercase letters which made no sense to Emilia. Amber had tried to stop herself from laughing as she explained that those random symbols were probably emojis that Emilia's phone wasn't advanced enough to interpret.

After a quick text back and another reply from Hugo, it was clear that the man was excited to be invited to an early Christmas feast.

Amber had noticed that Emilia often spoke about 'her friends' but only ever mentioned one by name: Hugo. She'd already surmised that Hugo was her only friend and guessed that Emilia was embellishing her language to give the impression she had more. Not that she could blame her, she suspected she would do the same.

Amber was looking forward to meeting him. She knew he had gone to school with Emilia and they'd remained close ever since. She got the feeling that he was slowly drifting away from Emilia with his new job and work colleagues, though, something that Emilia had half-heartedly referenced a few times.

She hoped that wasn't the case. It was obvious that he was all Emilia had and solely responsible for the tiny amount of socialising that she did. If he was no longer there, what would become of Emilia?

After her shower, Amber took longer than usual to choose an outfit to wear for dinner. She wanted to dress warmly, knowing that the snow had continued to fall and the short walk from the guesthouse would be cold. But she also wanted to wear her plunge-neck top. She tried to tell herself it was simply because it was comfortable, but she knew deep down she wanted to show off a little more skin to Emilia than she had in previous days.

It was hard to look sexy when you constantly wore at least four layers to keep the chill out.

I'm not dressing up for Emilia, I'm dressing up for me, she told herself for the sixth time.

"Is lying to yourself one of the first signs of madness?" she wondered aloud. "Or is it talking to yourself?"

She let out a breath and grabbed the plunge-neck top. She'd wear a scarf she had borrowed from Emilia when walking over to the main house. It smelt of Emilia's cosy scent, and she'd kept hold of it when they had returned.

She got dressed, checking her reflection in the bathroom mirror one last time before heading downstairs to put on her winter boots. It seemed crazy to have to lace up heavy boots for a tiny journey to the house, but it was necessary. There were so many things about life in a snowy climate that she'd never taken into consideration before.

At first, she'd thought it was inconvenient, but now it was a fact of life. If it meant spending time with Emilia, then she'd happily lace up heavy boots for a thirty-second journey.

Bright lights lit up the courtyard, and she saw a car pulling up on the tarmac. She glanced at the clock on the wall and realised she had spent a little longer on her fashion crisis than she'd hoped.

She headed outside, shoving her hands into her pockets to protect them from the cold. The car engine shut off, and the lights dimmed.

"Hallo! You must be Amber?" Hugo stepped out of the car and greeted her with a big smile.

"I am. And you must be Hugo? I've heard a lot about you."

They shook hands. Amber could instantly see why Emilia and Hugo were friends. He was lanky, what would be attractive to some in a wholly uncool, geeky way. His smile and his eyes were soft and kind. He instantly put her at ease.

"Have you been having a good time here in Sweden?" Hugo asked, his accent thick.

"Yes, it's been so much fun. We were at the Christmas market this morning, that's when Emilia decided to show me what a Swedish Christmas meal looks like."

"*Ja,* I hope you brought a second stomach." He

laughed. "I'm glad you have had a good time, despite the business problems."

"Problems?" Amber asked. She wondered if it was an error in translation or if he meant having to ruin a perfectly nice visit by talking about business.

Hugo hesitated. "Yes… Emilia and business, she won't…" He stopped and looked towards the house, panic and realisation in his eyes. "I mean. We—we should probably go inside."

All at once, Amber had a terrible suspicion she knew what Hugo was about to say. She also had a sinking feeling.

"Oh," she attempted to sound casual, "you mean that Emilia won't do business with us?"

"Precis." He smiled, relieved that she knew. Or so he thought.

"Because she refuses to ever talk about business," Amber guessed.

"Yes. She hates it so leaves it to her agent. But he doesn't do anything either. And so, nothing ever happens." Hugo chuckled, completely unaware that Amber's mood was spiralling.

She lied to me. Amber felt all the breath from her lungs vanish. *She's been lying to me all along. She just wanted me here… for what? For friendship? For… a laugh?*

"What are you two doing standing out here in the cold?" Emilia called from the porch.

Amber's eyes were wet with unshed tears. She couldn't believe she had been so stupid. And wasted so much time.

"When do you think you'll be ready to talk about the

contract, Emilia?" Amber shouted over to her. "Tonight? Tomorrow? Never?"

All the colour drained from Emilia's face. It was all the confirmation she needed.

"Oh… I think I…" Hugo trailed off, realising his mistake.

"Did you ever have any intention of signing the contract?" Amber asked.

Emilia hesitated for a moment before shaking her head.

At least she's honest, Amber thought.

The falling snow no longer felt cold. Amber didn't know if it was because of her white-hot rage, or due to the fact she was numb with shock.

"Just so you know, I'll be fired for this," Amber said. "And, to be honest, I would have preferred spending this time trying to find a new job rather than being here. I… I don't even know what to say."

She turned around and stalked back towards the guesthouse.

"Wait!" Emilia called.

She heard Hugo say something in Swedish but didn't turn around. She kicked off her boots once inside the kitchen and raced upstairs to her bedroom. After a few moments it was clear that neither of them were going to follow her, something to be thankful for.

She paced the room, wondering how her entire mood could be reversed in a matter of seconds. Emilia had no intention of ever signing the contract. Even Hugo knew that. It was only Amber who was stupid enough to think that it was a possibility. She'd been played. She didn't know why, but she knew that much.

She swiped at her tears with the back of her hand. There was no way she was going to sit down and eat dinner with Emilia now. She was too angry, and she didn't know what to say. She had a hundred questions but also didn't want to hear a single answer. Nothing Emilia could say could make it better.

She paused her pacing.

It was clear what she needed to do. There was no reason to stay. The best course of action was to put as much distance as possible between herself and Emilia.

She opened the wardrobe and started grabbing handfuls of clothes and throwing them onto the bed. She didn't know if there were any flights back to London, but she'd sleep in the airport if needed. Anything to be away from Emilia.

As soon as she told Bronwyn that she'd not only failed to get the contract signed but had also enjoyed an all-expenses paid holiday to Sweden on the company's time and money. She was a goner. She needed to get home and start looking for jobs.

She took a mental inventory of personal belongings on her desk at work, knowing that security would be called to accompany her out of the office the moment after Bronwyn had finished screaming.

It took Amber less than ten minutes to pack everything into her suitcase and get changed for travelling to the airport. The front door to the main house swung open just as she was putting her suitcase into the boot of her car.

"Amber, wait," Emilia pleaded.

"No, I have a flight to catch." She didn't know if that was true or not. For all she knew there could be no flights for the next twenty-four hours. It didn't matter, she needed to be away from the cosy little farmhouse that had been a home for the last couple of days. She was struck by the contrast between how little time she had spent at the Lund residence and how it already felt like a home away from home.

"I'm sorry I lied to you," Emilia said. She walked down the steps from the porch and towards the car.

"Look, Emilia, I really don't care right now. I need to go and try to save my job. People in the real world need those to have a roof over their head and to pay for food to live. I don't expect you to understand." Amber slammed the boot closed.

"I'm sorry, I just… I can't give my grandmother's work to some… some faceless corporation!" Emilia cried.

Amber stopped dead in her tracks to the car door. She stared coldly at Emilia.

"*I'm* not a faceless corporation. I thought I was your *friend*."

She got in the car and quickly reversed out of the courtyard and away from Emilia Lund forever.

26

A REALISATION

As AMBER's tail lights vanished in the distance, Hugo guided her back into the house. Emilia couldn't see where she was going through the tears filling her eyes.

"I'm so sorry," Hugo said. "I didn't know that she didn't know. I thought you were going to tell her."

"There was never a good time," Emilia heaved. "We… we were having so much fun. I didn't want to ruin that. I should have told her. I just… I just couldn't."

Hugo walked them over to the sofa and sat Emilia down. He sat beside her and put his arm around her. Emilia appreciated the gesture but couldn't help but feel that it wasn't as comforting as when Amber did the same.

Nothing felt the same now that Amber had left, especially because Emilia knew that she had left and would never return.

"She was here for work, Em," Hugo whispered.

"Maybe at first," Emilia agreed, "but then we connected. We were *friends*."

"Maybe you thought so."

Emilia turned her face into his chest and let the tears flow freely. She was sure that Amber was her friend. What other explanation could there be for the last couple of days? Why did things have to be business or friendship? Why couldn't business become friendship instead?

Did people who weren't friends cuddle on the sofa? She didn't think so. But then there was so much about Amber that was still a mystery to her. Now it seemed it would forever be a mystery.

"I'm never going to see her again," Emilia whispered, the realisation of the fact crashing over her again and again.

"I'm sure she'll calm down," Hugo tried to reassure her. "She's just upset because she thinks you lied to her."

"I did," Emilia confessed. "I wanted a friend so badly that I lied to get her here. And then carried on lying to her to keep her here. I'm a horrible, terrible person."

Hugo's arm around her tightened. "You're not either of those things. She'll come around."

"She won't." Emilia shook her head and pulled back. "She won't. I lied to her, and now she will be so angry at me. She said she was going to lose her job. Because of me."

A fresh wave of tears overcame her at that thought. She'd ruined Amber's career just because she wanted a friend. Because she was incapable of making friends in the conventional way, she'd had to con Amber to come and stay with her and befriend her.

"Maybe you could… sign that contract?" Hugo suggested.

She shook her head vigorously. "No. I couldn't do that to my grandmother. They will ruin the books. And I don't know enough about business to stop them. I could be signing my life away. I… I can't trust them."

"But you trust Amber, right?" he asked.

"Yes. But Amber isn't the boss. No. I could never sign that contract."

Hugo nodded. "I understand."

He looked at a loss, like someone wanting to offer comfort but unable to find any to give. She couldn't blame him. She'd made a complete mess of things, and there was no redemption to be had.

Amber would never want to talk to her again. Even if she did, the distance between them wasn't an easy thing to overcome. It's not like they would happen to see each other out shopping one day.

Emilia's throat closed up at the thought that she'd never see Amber's beautiful smile again. Or feel her soft, warm body against hers as they spoke in whispered tones well after bedtime. She'd never hear the warm chuckle fall from her lips when they joked or Emilia said something that she found amusing.

Most of all, she'd no longer feel the butterflies tossing and turning in her stomach whenever Amber was near.

Her eyes widened. She slapped her hand over her gasp.

"What?" Hugo looked panicked. He looked over to the kitchen. "Did you leave the oven on?"

"How… how do you know if you… love someone?" she asked.

He frowned. "Like… love? Do you think?"

' She sat up straight and nodded her head. "I think I might. I've only just put the pieces together now. How do you know?"

Hugo looked helpless. "I don't know. I suppose you want to be with that person all the time, you can't stop thinking about them." He paused. "Are you sure you mean love? Do you mean like a friend?"

Emilia thought about it, but in her heart she knew it was more than friendship. She felt very differently towards Amber than she did towards Hugo, or anyone else for that matter.

She touched her lips with the tips of her fingers, imagining they were Amber's lips. A wave of heat crashed over her. It was unmistakable.

"I think I fell for her," she whispered. "No, no. I know I did."

She walked in front of the window, staring out into the darkness. "I've never really been that interested in boys. I mean, there was Nils and Erik… I didn't care for them even half as much as I care for Amber. Maybe I'm bisexual, like she is?"

"She is bisexual?" Hugo asked.

"Yes." She wrapped her arms around herself.

"Are you sure you—"

"I'm sure," she cut him off. Whatever he was about to say was irrelevant. Her realisation of her feelings may have come on suddenly and without warning. Or perhaps they had been building for a while, she'd just been too swept away in them to realise what they were.

It seemed ridiculous, but she knew her heart. She had fallen for Amber.

She took a deep, shaky breath as she stared out into the blackness.

"And now I'll never see her again."

27

BACK TO WORK

"You look absolutely terrible," Caroline said as she handed her a takeaway coffee mug.

"Thanks so much." Amber knew she looked bad, but she didn't need confirmation from her supposed best friend on the matter.

"Have you slept?"

"I sure did. In Copenhagen Airport," Amber replied, taking a sip of coffee and closing her eyes as the scorching liquid filled her mouth. It was the simple pleasures that were going to get her through what would no doubt be one of the worst moments of her life.

"Sounds nice. What's the star rating there?" Caroline sipped her own drink and looked around the bustling coffee shop. "Let's find somewhere quieter, we can probably find a quiet corner in the station."

Amber nodded. Morning rush hour in a London café was nowhere to have a serious conversation. Caroline may have been flippant, but she also knew that Amber wasn't in the habit of texting her at eight in the morning to tell her that her life was ruined, and that she needed her best friend immediately.

Light rain fell from the sky as they weaved in and out of streams of commuters trying to get to their respective offices. Amber was relieved that it was rain and not snow. Snow brought London to a complete standstill. And now it reminded her of Emilia.

They ducked into Waterloo Station and walked up to the top level to get away from the crowds of people. They sat at a table outside a restaurant that didn't open until the late afternoon.

"So, what's happened? I see that she's not a murderer," Caroline said.

"No, but she is a liar," Amber replied bitterly. "She had no intention of signing the contract. No intention of doing business with us at all. It was all a lie."

Caroline looked as confused as Amber felt. "Then why did she want you to go over there?"

"I've no idea." Amber had racked her brains during her sleepless night at the airport but couldn't fathom why Emilia had told the lie she had. It didn't help that just thinking about Emilia caused her heart to clench in pain.

"There wasn't some kind of translation issue?"

"No, she speaks perfect English. She knows words you don't—"

"Hey."

"She definitely lied to me. She pretended that she did business only with people she knew well, but she had no intention of even talking about it. She called me a faceless corporation." That admission had slipped out. She hadn't intended to focus on that point, but her sleep-deprived brain had latched onto it again and again. She couldn't believe that was what Emilia thought of her.

"Ouch." Caroline placed her hand on hers. "What's the next step?"

Amber exhaled a deep breath. "Now… I lose my job. I'm not supposed to be back for a couple of days, so whenever I get the courage to go into the office… I do. Then I tell Bronwyn what happened, and she fires me."

"Is there any chance you can convince her to keep you on? Appeal to her Christmas spirit?"

Amber gave her a look.

"Right. Yeah. The devil, I remember. I'm so sorry, I wish there was something I could do to help."

"It's okay. I just needed to see a friendly face. I rushed out of there yesterday evening, missed the last flight of the day, and had to sleep in the airport. But I didn't sleep because I was so angry at myself for falling for her lies. And then I got the first flight this morning, which was expensive, and I don't know if the company might refuse to pay it and deduct it from my last salary. Oh, Caz, everything is such a mess."

Caroline didn't reply. Amber looked up at her friend who was staring off into the distance.

"Hello? Earth to Caroline?"

"Look." Caroline pointed towards the enormous television screen above the departure boards that normally showed either the news or advertising.

"Oh no…" Amber's heart sank. The television showed a live news report of a vehicle attack in the London Bridge area. She waited as the ticker tape along the bottom of the screen scrolled around. Early reports were that there had been multiple casualties. Police were still hunting for the suspect.

"Terrifying," Caroline breathed.

"Yeah." Amber's problems suddenly felt tiny in comparison to what was happening a short distance away.

"Nowhere is safe," Caroline whispered.

"No, it's not. And this is the second terrorist incident on London Bridge," Amber said.

"And there was the one in Westminster."

"And the one at the Tube station," Amber remembered.

Caroline's brow furrowed. "Where was that again?"

"Wasn't it Parsons Green?"

"Yes, that was it. Isn't it terrible that there have been so many that we start to forget them?" Caroline shook her head. "They've become the new normal." She shivered at the thought.

"True. But, like they say, we can't let the terrorists win. Right?" Amber said.

It was something that most Londoners found themselves saying at one point or another. No one was about to stop living their life because of cowardly terrorism.

"Damn right," Caroline said. "I'll still be out tonight."

"If you're buying, I'll be with you," Amber said with a faint laugh, the emptiness of her bank account already playing on her mind.

"You know you have a place on my sofa if you need it," Caroline said. "You won't, though, because you'll be fine. You're great at your job, and you'll be snapped up by a better employer in no time. But I won't let you be homeless, so don't worry about silly things like that."

Amber reached across the table and pulled Caroline into a hug. She knew she was blessed to have such a great friend, and such a wonderful group of friends in general. If anything went wrong, even though the thought was mortifying, she'd be supported. She didn't want to mess up her life so badly that she needed saving, but the safety net was appreciated.

"Thank you. I can't tell you how much I appreciate that." She pulled away, her eyes looking at the news report. "I can't watch that anymore. I think I better get into the office and face my fate."

"Okay. Let me know what happens."

They stood up and hugged once more. Caroline wished her luck before waving her off, ordering her to be careful. They both knew that being careful had nothing to do with it. It was a sad state of affairs that the world they lived in now meant the risk of terror attacks. It could happen at any time and to anyone.

But Amber was more concerned about Bronwyn than any terrorist. Why spend time worrying about something that would probably never happen when something much more tangible was lurking right around the corner?

Tom looked at Amber and then at his watch and then back at Amber again. It was a pointless exercise which caused her to sigh at his ridiculous dramatics.

"I thought you were out for a few more days," he finally said.

"I was, but now I'm back." She placed her bag on her desk and looked towards Bronwyn's closed office door.

"She's out," Tom explained before she could ask. "She'll be back later this afternoon. Not sure when."

Amber rolled her eyes. She'd spent the last half-hour walking up and down the street to try to find the courage to come in and be fired, and now Bronwyn didn't even have the courtesy to be there.

She wondered what to do next. Should she leave again and come back later? Take the cowardly way out and leave a letter? No, that would just result in a later phone call to pick over the remains of what had happened and attempt to justify the cowardly letter.

And she didn't really want to quit. She didn't want to leave at all, not yet. Not while the employment market was so quiet. If she could hang on at Walker Clay for a few more weeks, everything might just work out okay.

The chance of Bronwyn giving her another chance was slim. But there was a chance, and her bank account and upcoming bills were begging her to take it.

She looked at her in tray. It was bulging with post from the last few days.

Might find the next Harry Potter in that lot, she thought to herself. *The only thing that might save me now.*

"Are you going to sit down or hover there all day?" Tom asked.

"Seeing as you asked so nicely." She put her coat on the back of her chair and sat down.

Her heart was thumping against her rib cage. The day had turned into a ticking time bomb. Bronwyn would unexpectedly return to the office at who knew when, and

Amber was going to have to sit at her desk and wait for that horrible moment. Her only hope was to find something incredible in her work pile or her inbox.

Which was about as likely as London having a white Christmas.

It really was turning into the day from hell. She'd hardly slept, her neck ached from the uncomfortable airport chairs, London was under attack again, and now she was waiting for the axe to fall. And on top of all of that, her brain kept unhelpfully providing her with images of Emilia.

She picked up the first hefty manuscript on the pile and skimmed the poorly worded query letter. She'd be glad when the day was over.

28

TO THE RESCUE

THE WALK into town took longer than usual. It wasn't the fresh snow that slowed Emilia down, it was her mood. For the first time in years, getting out of bed had seemed like a chore.

She was often up early and happy to get the day started. In fact, even that morning she had woken up early and been excited to get out of bed until she remembered that Amber was gone, and the events of the previous evening came back to her like a ton weight on her chest.

She'd pulled the blanket up and over her head and allowed her tears to fall again. It was another four hours before she finally got herself out of bed. She'd nearly gone right back when she'd seen her ghastly reflection in the bathroom mirror.

Eventually her stomach had complained of hunger. She couldn't face the mess in the kitchen, she'd left the partially cooked food out when she'd gone to bed the evening before. There was nothing for it but to go out and get something to eat from town. No matter how terrible she looked.

While she was getting dressed she thought about what she would get to eat at her favourite bakery, only to realise that she would be revisiting the place where she had first met Amber.

The walk usually took around twenty-five minutes. She didn't know how long she had been walking, but the fact that the cold air had seeped through her jacket told her that it had been at least double that.

She wondered when the tears and lethargy would let up. Or if they ever would. The last time she had felt this terrible was when she was eleven years old and her perfect home life had started to unravel.

This was different, of course. The end of a friendship was nothing like the loss of loved ones, but the empty hole in her heart felt the same. And she felt just as confused and lost as she had done then.

It was as if her brain were only half awake. And that half was manic. The part that was asleep was shrouded in a fog that she couldn't shake.

She couldn't remember Hugo leaving the night before. She knew they had spoken for a long time and that he had forced her to eat some toasted bread. But as the night went on and her tears refused to subside, the memories became hazy.

She wished that Amber was there, not just because she wanted to apologise but because Amber somehow knew how to fix things. Amber knew when she was falling off a cliff and knew exactly what to say to help.

Her breath caught in her throat. She needed to stop thinking that way. Amber was gone. She'd driven her away with lies and she wouldn't ever be returning.

She felt the wind of a passing car and realised that she was walking in the road and nearing the middle of town. She stepped up onto the walkway and sped up thanks to the gritted area.

A few minutes later she walked into the bakery. As she'd expected, her heart sank as she looked at the table where she'd had her first meeting with Amber. A woman with a baby sat there now.

Emilia turned away and walked to the counter. She was so hungry that her body was shaking, but her appetite was missing. She hated how her body was falling apart, hated feeling so completely broken. Even if she did deserve it.

The waitress greeted her and asked to take her order. She quickly ordered her usual sandwich, cheese and ham. Plain and filling.

The television behind the counter was showing images of blue flashing lights and police, but they didn't look like the Swedish Polis.

"*Vad har hänt?*" She asked.

"*En terroristattack i London.*" The waitress lifted the portable device to the counter so Emilia could see the small screen better. She carried on talking, explaining what had happened, but Emilia couldn't hear anything except the rushing sound that filled her ears.

People were dead. Many more were injured. A madman had driven into them, on purpose. It was utterly unthinkable. Emilia couldn't comprehend why someone would ever do such a thing, and certainly not at a Christmas market.

Suddenly she couldn't remember what Amber had told her about her job. She couldn't recall where the office was based, how Amber got to work. All she knew was that Amber had a flight the previous evening and was now in London.

Probably right in the middle of the attack.

What if she's dead? Emilia panicked. *Or injured. Does she have anyone to look after her? What if she is hurt and alone?*

She asked for her sandwich to go and handed over some money. She grabbed the paper bag and hurried from the bakery, not bothering to put her gloves back on. She crossed the town square, wondering whether it was best to go into the travel agency or the taxi office first.

The tell-tale blackness of an impending panic attack swarmed in her vision.

She paused and took a deep breath to calm herself. Amber needed her, and she needed to think clearly. After a couple of seconds, the blackness left as quickly as it had arrived. She blinked a few times to clear her vision and her mind.

Get the plane booked first, she thought. *Then get the taxi home to get your passport.*

She was relieved that she'd always kept her passport up to date. She told herself she kept it in case she ever decided to realise her dream of travelling the world. In reality, she knew that would never happen. She'd never even considered going to Copenhagen or Stockholm, never mind farther afield.

It would be the first time she'd ever used her passport.

First stop, London.

29

FIRED

IN THE BACK of her mind, Amber knew she'd never find the holy grail to employment in her in tray. She'd looked several times just to be sure. Once the inevitability of it all had set in, she'd gone out to get a huge share bag of chocolate and proceeded to eat it herself as she waited for the end.

As it happened, the end arrived at ten minutes to five.

Bronwyn raised an eyebrow as she noticed Amber. She silently pointed to her office. Amber grabbed a few more pieces of chocolate and shoved them in her mouth before following Bronwyn.

"Close the door."

She closed the door and stood behind the visitor seat.

"You're back early," Bronwyn noted. "And judging from the fact you look like your dog died, I'm assuming you have failed to return with a signed contract."

"Emilia Lund had no intention of signing a contract, she lied to me," Amber said.

"And why would she do that?" Bronwyn asked,

sounding mildly interested. Amber couldn't blame her, it was the number one question on her mind, too.

"I've no idea," she replied honestly. Even now, after a few more hours with the quandary, she still couldn't figure it out.

"Well, you know what this means," Bronwyn said.

Amber had already decided that she wouldn't be pleading for her job. It was pointless to appeal to Bronwyn's heart, as it was questionable whether or not she had one.

"Clear your desk out. I'm going to assume I won't have to call security?" Bronwyn asked with a sigh, as if she were the one hard done by.

"You won't. I want to thank you for the opportunity of working here," Amber said politely. She knew that she needed to butter Bronwyn up as she was probably still unaware of the cost of the last-minute flight home that she'd charged to the company.

"HR will call you in a couple of days to finalise anything that needs to be discussed." Bronwyn picked up an envelope from her in tray and ripped it open.

Amber assumed that was the end of the discussion and left the office, thankful for the calm dismissal. Having sat close to Bronwyn's office, she'd heard some eruptions in the past.

She went straight to the stationery cupboard and picked up an archive box. Luckily, she'd been slowly taking her personal belongings home for the last few months. She had a few items left, but nothing she'd be sad to lose. They were mainly there so it didn't look like she was jumping the sinking ship, which she now wished she had done months ago. To think that she could have a career at Walker Clay was foolish. She was never going to win Bronwyn over.

She dropped the empty box on her desk and started to pack up the few things she had.

"Oh, bad luck," Tom said without feeling.

"Yeah, thanks."

"I won't see you, so I suppose I should say Merry Christmas now," he continued.

She was about to reply when her phone rang. She nearly ignored it until she noticed it was reception.

"Amber Tate," she answered.

"Hi Amber, I have someone in reception for you."

Amber frowned. "I don't have a meeting scheduled."

"She's very insistent," the receptionist whispered. "She says her name is Emilia Lund."

Amber blinked. "She's… *in* reception? Not on the phone?"

"She's standing in front of me."

"I'll be down in a few seconds." She slammed the phone down, quickly tipped the rest of her belongings into the box and slid the lid on.

"Problem?" Tom asked.

"Have a great Christmas, Tom," she said as she threw her coat on and picked up the box and her handbag.

She rushed through the office, all thoughts of how she would spend her last moments at Walker Clay temporarily pushed to one side. She'd pictured her departure involving a slow walk, waving forlornly at colleagues. A last run of her hand along the new release shelf, knowing that her stream of free books would soon be coming to an end.

Instead, she was racing towards the elevators to take her to reception where there had surely been some kind of mistake. Emilia couldn't be there. Could she? Why would she be there?

Has she changed her mind?

It seemed impossible. Emilia hated leaving her house. The city often sent her into a spiral of panic. She couldn't possibly be standing in the reception of a publishing company in London. It was all of Emilia's terrors in one.

Which meant it must be an imposter, or a huge mistake.

Amber's foot tapped with irritation. The elevator had never taken longer to get to the ground floor.

The doors had hardly opened when she forced her way through them.

She spotted her immediately, huddled on the edge of one of the leather sofas. Her face was drawn, and she looked like she had been in the midst of a serious panic for many hours.

What happened? Amber wondered. *Has something happened to Hugo?*

She dropped her box onto one of the tables in reception. "Emilia?"

The Swede jumped to her feet. "Amber," she breathed, pulling her into a hug. "You're alive! You're… you're okay. You are okay, aren't you?"

Amber was suddenly pushed back as Emilia's eyes ran over her body in search of any apparent injury.

Amber had questions of her own. "What on earth are you doing here?"

"I saw the attack. I was so scared." Emilia, seemingly satisfied that Amber wasn't injured, resumed her hug.

Amber loosely placed her arms around Emilia, still confused. She made eye contact with the receptionist who clearly thought Emilia was barking mad.

"What attack?" she asked.

"The terrorist attack, it's all over the news."

"Since when do you watch the news?" Amber couldn't understand how on earth Emilia would know about the London Bridge incident or why she would think that she had been caught up in it.

"It happened in London, and you're in London," Emilia continued.

"London has the same population as Sweden," Amber pointed out.

"And I was so scared," Emilia said, completely ignoring Amber's words. "I saw the attack on the news."

She realised then that Emilia was in shock. It wasn't surprising, considering that Emilia had gone from full-on recluse to taking an unexpected trip to another country, all while apparently thinking that Amber was dead.

She tightened her grip around Emilia. "I'm fine, everything is fine." She found that her rage was fading now that she held the shivering woman in her arms.

"Unfortunately, these things happen in big cities now," she told Emilia.

"Then why would you live here?"

She wasn't about to get into a conversation about quality of life and not letting terror win, not to mention the economy of jobs. She had too many other questions, and she wasn't entirely sure that Emilia would take in her response anyway.

"How did you even find me?" Amber asked.

"The taxi driver wouldn't take me to London Bridge," Emilia said, "so I asked him to take me to Walker Clay Publishing. His phone knew where it was."

As Amber started to piece things together, she realised that Emilia wasn't dressed for a London winter. She was bundled up like a toddler. She was dressed for Sweden.

Amber looked around them.

No bags. Did she? No, surely not.

"Did… did you come straight here? Do you have any luggage?"

"I thought you were dead; I didn't have time to find my suitcase," Emilia said.

"When is your flight home?" Amber asked.

Emilia remained silent, still clinging to her like a lifeline.

"Right, okay," Amber said. "Let's… well, let's start with getting out of here."

She extricated herself from Emilia's grip and picked up her archive box. Emilia fell into step beside her as she walked out of Walker Clay for the very last time.

The fear of her unemployment had taken a backseat to the realisation that Emilia had dropped everything and flown to London at a moment's notice. She hadn't brought a stitch of clothing with her and was still wearing her thick, woolly gloves and scarf.

She couldn't abandon her. Emilia might have been a hundred and fifty years old when it came to darning socks, keeping a house, and cooking dinner, but she was a wide-eyed child when it came to a foreign city.

"I was so scared," Emilia repeated.

"I know. But everything is okay now," Amber said.

There was no point in being angry at Emilia, nor in having an in-depth conversation with her. She was in state of shock, and no matter what had come before, she needed Amber to look after her.

Amber handed the archive box to Emilia and got her house keys out of her handbag. She was trying to remember what state she had left her apartment in, considering she hadn't been there since the day she left for Sweden. She hoped there was nothing rotting in the bin. Or the fridge.

She wasn't the tidiest of people. Certainly nothing like Emilia. Not that there was anything to be done about it now.

She opened the door and gestured for Emilia to step inside.

She followed her in and closed the door behind her, applying the deadbolt. She lived in a nice area, but it always paid to be careful. When she turned around, Emilia stood in the same spot, looking around the tiny apartment and holding the archive box.

"Let me take that." Amber took the box and placed it on her small dining table. It couldn't hold more than three dinner plates, but it was perfect for partially balancing a cardboard box on.

"This is where you live?" Emilia asked, the first thing she had said since they left the Walker Clay office.

"Yes."

"It's very small."

Amber shook her head in disbelief. "Yes, it is. But it's all you've got, so you'll have to struggle on." She took a few steps into the kitchen and started to make herself some coffee.

"I'm sorry, that was rude," Emilia said.

"Yes, it was. Can I get you coffee? It's not like Swedish coffee, but it will have to do."

"Yes, please. I am sorry. Your house is lovely."

"Apartment," Amber corrected. She didn't need to, but she felt like being petty. She couldn't believe that Emilia had just turned up. The reason for her unemployment had turned up unexpectedly on the very day of her unemployment and needed her help. It was a little too much to take in, especially with exhaustion curling around her.

"Are you angry with me?" Emilia whispered.

"What makes you say that?"

"You're throwing things around."

Amber paused making drinks. She had been a bit heavy-handed.

"It's just been a bad day at work, I'm not angry at you."

Half true, she thought.

"You can stay here tonight, until you get yourself sorted out and can go home," Amber explained. She turned and looked at Emilia. She looked wretched. Pale, shaking, her eyes wild and lost.

"You can have the bed, I'll sleep on the sofa," Amber

said. She pinched the bridge of her nose. She wanted to be angry, but she just couldn't. "And tonight, we'll be ordering takeaway food and watching movies. And there will be no complaining about either."

Emilia quickly nodded. She seemed to reading loud and clear how frustrated Amber was.

She turned and made the coffee. Instant coffee. Emilia would hate it. Everyone in Sweden seemed to be a massive coffee snob. Amber's lips curled up in amusement. It would be amusing watching Emilia pretend that it didn't taste like dishwater to her.

As she stirred the drinks, she realised she had a million questions that she wanted to ask. How had Emilia managed to navigate Copenhagen Airport without having a complete meltdown? Where had she flown into in London? What was her plan to get home? Had she eaten?

That last one was more urgent than the others. As annoyed as she was, she couldn't leave Emilia to starve.

"Are you hungry?"

There was a long pause.

"No," Emilia whispered uncertainly.

Clearly a yes, Amber thought.

She opened the cupboard door and pulled out a box of biscuits. They weren't homemade and tied up with ribbon as she imagined Emilia would have presented them, but they'd do.

"Go and sit on the sofa," she instructed, knowing that otherwise Emilia would simply stand in the middle of the room.

She debated whether or not to take the biscuits out of the cardboard box and place them on a plate. Shaking her head, she tucked the box under her arm and grabbed the two mugs.

She placed everything on the coffee table and sat as far away from Emilia on the sofa as possible. Not easy, considering her small apartment demanded an equally small sofa.

Out of the corner of her eye she noted that Emilia was still wearing her thick winter coat and scarf. The gloves had been shoved into her pockets.

"Help yourself to biscuits," Amber said.

She reached forward to grab the remote control and turned on the television. Images of the London Bridge attack immediately filled the screen, and she could feel Emilia tense.

She changed the channel, then again, and then again. She was never usually home at this time and all she could find were programs about people wanting to move to the country, or panels of women speaking to some celebrity she couldn't identify.

Ordinarily she would have opened Netflix and dived into one of her many box-set series, but she knew it was just a matter of time before one of them cracked and started to speak. She was fairly sure that it wasn't going to be her.

Emilia hesitantly reached forward and picked up the coffee mug.

Amber kept channel-hopping.

Emilia opened the biscuit box and started to nibble on a digestive.

Amber watched her in the reflection of the television. She looked so lost and helpless.

It's like trying to be angry with a puppy, she thought.

"Are you okay? Can I get you anything?" Amber finally asked. She was still angry, but if she could stop Emilia from looking so broken, then maybe she could stop focusing on her.

"You've been very kind. Considering everything," Emilia said.

"Well, I can't leave you out on the streets," Amber sighed.

"I *am* sorry."

Amber turned to face her. "What are you sorry about, Emilia?" she challenged.

Emilia swallowed nervously. She placed the coffee mug back in the table.

"For lying to you about my intention to sign the contract. For making you come to Sweden and hang out with me. For coming here and being a nuisance." Emilia paused, her eyes lit up as if she'd had an epiphany. "I should stay at a hotel. I came to see if you were okay, and now I'm in the way."

The idea of Emilia going to a hotel didn't sit well with Amber. She could just imagine Emilia wandering into some illegal drug den. Or a human-trafficking circle. Those things surely existed in London somewhere, and if they did, Emilia would probably manage to find them.

"No." Amber shook her head. "It's fine, you can stay with me. I'm still angry at you, but at least this way I can keep an eye on you. Besides, you don't have any clothes... or a toothbrush... or, well, anything." She let out a deep breath. "What were you thinking, Emilia? I don't get it."

Emilia look down at the sofa between them. "I wasn't thinking. I saw the news, and I immediately assumed that you were in trouble. I didn't stop panicking about it until I saw you at your office."

Amber couldn't imagine the fear of seeing a terrorist attack on the news, something that Emilia had probably never seen before, and thinking someone she knew was in the middle of it all. It was sweet that Emilia had dropped everything and come running. Even if she had done so in the most disorganised way possible.

"So, you just… booked a flight?" Amber asked.

"Yes. To Heathrow. The lady at the travel agency said there were two others, but I'd heard of that one." Emilia finally looked up. Colour was returning to her cheeks, to Amber's relief.

"And then you… got a taxi?"

"Yes."

"You tried to get him to take you to the middle of an ongoing terrorist incident?"

"Yes, but he said he wouldn't. I said you might be there, but he still said no. He said it might be dangerous and I should stay indoors. He didn't understand at all."

"I bet he didn't," Amber muttered. She tossed her eternal gratitude to the taxi driver who had done his best to keep Emilia safe.

She still wasn't sure she understood. Emilia, who toyed with her feelings and her time, had flown to the UK and tried to walk into the centre of hell to try to… what? Save her?

It was too much to think about right now. Amber was too stressed following her own day from hell to try to process what on earth was going on in Emilia's head. She needed time, she needed to process everything that had happened.

"Let's watch a movie," Amber suggested.

She fired up Netflix. She was sure she could find a sweet romcom that would be innocuous enough.

"Okay," Emilia said. "As long as you're sure I should stay? I can get a hotel…"

"No, there aren't any around here," Amber joked. "All booked up. You're staying here. Where I can keep an eye on you, or you'll be jetting off to Tokyo next."

Emilia breathed out a small chuckle.

Amber selected a movie and snuggled down into the sofa. She could feel her eyelids getting heavy and doubted that she'd see more than the first ten minutes before she fell asleep. Which was exactly what she needed.

After some rest, she'd be able to deal with the mystery that was Emilia Lund.

30

RESTLESS IN LONDON

EMILIA KNELT on Amber's bed, resting on the headboard as she looked out of the window. It was nearing midnight and she couldn't sleep. She'd been surprised to see that so many other people were up and about at this late hour.

Train tracks ran near Amber's home, and the illuminated carriages showed many people on board. Emilia watched in fascination as trains passed in both directions. Multiple carriages, so many people.

At first she couldn't understand why so many people were still awake. It was midnight. Most people in her tiny town were tucked up in bed at midnight.

Even on the street below, there were people out. Some were walking alone, some in pairs, or even groups. Some were eating from takeaway boxes, some on the phone.

Emilia watched all of them with fascination.

She'd always known that people outside Malmö lived different lives. She wasn't naïve enough to think that everyone was just like her. She knew that Hugo was nothing like her, and her books told her a thousand tales of other worlds. But to see it with her own eyes, in borrowed pyjamas and overlooking the streets of Greater London, it was a revelation.

She'd counted over two hundred people in the past five minutes. Her guess was not quite accurate as the trains passing made it difficult to count, but she knew that there were at least two hundred people living other lives, lives that she couldn't even begin to comprehend, just outside of Amber's window.

It was starting to dawn on her just how small her world was.

Amber had looked at her like she was insane to think that she had been caught up in the terrorist attack. As if the mere facts that it happened in London and Amber lived and worked in London weren't anywhere near enough to cause concern.

Apparently, terrorist attacks were a thing now. Not some nightmare creation of a crime author, but a reality that people lived through.

She wondered just how out of touch with the world she was. Cutting herself off from the hurt and horror of the outside world had seemed like a good idea all those years ago, but now she didn't recognise the world she lived in.

It was like she had been released from a long stint in prison and was having to readjust to the outside world.

Maybe she was waking up from her self-enforced solitude.

Perhaps that was the reason that she'd taken the bizarre step to fly to London.

She leaned her head on the cold window. She couldn't

believe she'd boarded a plane with nothing but a chocolate bar in her pocket and assumed that she would be able to find Amber in a city of millions of people.

If the taxi driver had taken her to London Bridge, what would have happened to her? Where would she be now? Finding Amber had been a stroke of luck, nothing more. She'd taken a risk and somehow everything had worked out, but it just as easily could have been a disaster.

Her warm breath fogged up the window. She tried to contain the panic welling within her.

Sheer dumb luck had taken her to Walker Clay and into Amber's arms. And thank goodness, because without Amber's kindness, she didn't know where she would have ended up.

Amber would have been perfectly within her rights to turn her away, to want nothing more to do with her. Luckily for Emilia, Amber had a big heart.

She didn't know if she had Amber's forgiveness. She suspected she didn't even deserve it.

They hadn't spoken much throughout the evening. Amber had seemed content to watch movies back to back, pausing only to order food which was delivered to the door by a man in a crash helmet.

They'd eaten in silence before Amber announced that she wanted an early night. She'd shown Emilia the bedroom, thrust a pair of pyjamas into her hand, and said goodnight.

That had been two hours ago.

She peeled her forehead away from the glass and looked towards the closed bedroom door. She wondered if Amber was asleep out on the couch.

She'd been in shock for most of the evening. She knew she had stumbled her way through some kind of an apology, but also knew it wasn't enough.

Sleep wasn't coming anytime soon, and she was feeling claustrophobic in the cramped room. Not that she would tell Amber that her bedroom was small. She'd learnt that lesson on arrival. Sometimes her mouth went into motion before her brain.

The more she thought about it, the more she knew she had to leave the room. The air was becoming warm and thick, and she was starting to feel the edges of panic taking her over.

She pushed away the bedding and got out of bed. She decided to sit in the dining area, far away from Amber. Well, as far as possible in the small space. At least it wouldn't be the bedroom anymore.

She tiptoed across the room and opened the bedroom door as slowly as she could. Upon entering the living space, she noticed that Amber was awake. She was laying on the sofa with the sheets she had pulled out of the cupboard covering her.

Her eyes were open, staring at the ceiling.

"Do you need something?" Amber asked without looking at her.

"No. I…" She reminded herself to not talk about her dislike of the cramped space. "Couldn't sleep. And I wanted to apologise and explain."

"It's fine. You apologised." Amber sounded dejected.

"But you didn't accept my apology," Emilia said.

Amber stopped looking at the ceiling and made eye

contact with her. "Do you *need* me to accept your apology?"

"I'd like you to. I…"

I'd like us to be friends, she thought.

"Look, Emilia, maybe I will. But not right now. I've had a really bad day. Getting no sleep and then getting fired, and then you turning up—"

"You were fired?" Emilia couldn't believe that Amber's boss had done something so cruel so close to Christmas. She knew Amber had thought it was a possibility, but she'd assumed she was exaggerating.

"Yep."

"But… it's nearly Christmas." Emilia sat on the coffee table and looked at Amber. "Who would do that so near to Christmas?"

"Bronwyn Walker," Amber answered. "She's evil. She's like the story of Martin Martinsson, completely absorbed with herself with an evil plan in mind."

Emilia blinked in surprise. Not only had Amber mentioned one of her grandmother's stories, but she'd also picked a less common one that was rarely included in the translations. She'd obviously remembered it in between all the other books they had read in Swedish.

"Except Martin was eventually redeemed by baking the bread for the school. Bronwyn would probably set the school on fire because she wanted to build herself a home there," Amber continued.

"You… know that story?" Emilia asked.

"I know all of your grandmother's stories," Amber said. "Like I know that in 'The Gift That Keeps on

Giving,' the character of Maria is actually your mother when she was a child."

Emilia froze. "That… that's not true."

"Yes, it is." Amber sat up and pulled the sheets around her. "Maria is an outgoing and fun child, but she is always getting herself into trouble. She's the only character in all the collection that never gets their comeuppance. Her crimes are small, but other characters who perform similar crimes get punished. Maria never does. She's treated differently, she's special. Because she's the author's daughter."

Emilia couldn't believe what she was hearing. She'd heard the story a hundred times, read it a hundred more. Neither her mother nor her grandmother had ever said a word about Maria.

"I'm sorry, have I upset you?" Amber asked.

Emilia glanced up at her and shook her head. "No, no. I'm just… surprised. I didn't know that."

She wondered why no one had told her. Was it a secret? Or was it so obvious that they assumed she would know? Either way, finding out now was a shock.

"I'm sorry, perhaps I shouldn't have said anything," Amber said.

"No, it's okay. I… I'm glad I know." She looked around the darkened room. "Maybe…" she trailed off, wondering if she should ask. She'd already put Amber out so much. Was it right to ask for favours now?

"Maybe what?" Amber asked.

"I… can't sleep. And it seems that you can't either," Emilia said. "Maybe we could sit together and watch some more television?"

Amber's eyebrows raised. "*You* want to watch television?"

Emilia shrugged. "It's kind of comforting."

Amber reached for the remote control. She patted the seat next to her, and Emilia gratefully sat on the sofa. The glow from the TV illuminated the room. Amber pressed some buttons, and in a short amount of time an old black-and-white movie was starting.

Amber placed the remote control back on the coffee table and leaned back. She looked at Emilia for a moment before reaching behind herself and unfolding the sheets.

"It's cold," Amber said simply as she wrapped some of the bedding around them both.

"Thank you," Emilia said. She knew she didn't deserve the kindness, but she would gladly accept it.

AN ADORABLE NIGHTMARE

AMBER FELT herself slowly returning to consciousness. The sun was streaming in through the window. She could hear soft, unidentifiable sounds filtering through the apartment, and she could feel a warmth that could only be attributed to sleeping next to someone.

That last point caused her to open her eyes in surprise.

She was half-laying on top of Emilia Lund.

The sounds were the cutest half-snore she'd ever heard emanating from the body beneath her.

Her sleep-deprived brain raced to catch up with events. She remembered sleeping in the airport, flying home, seeing Caroline, the live news of the attack. She swallowed. Then there was half a day of work, Bronwyn firing her, Emilia turning up at the office.

Talk about a hectic day, she thought.

She gently moved herself away from Emilia. It was obvious that she had been the one to instigate the sleepy hug. It wasn't as if Emilia possessed the strength to lift Amber and place her on top of her.

She felt guilty that her feelings had risen and demonstrated themselves while Emilia had innocently slept. Then again, she had to pull herself away from Emilia's legs that had intertwined with her own. Maybe it wasn't as one-sided as she thought.

No, don't go there, she told herself.

Thinking for even a moment that Emilia might want more than friendship led to heartache. She didn't want to forget that Emilia had tricked her, lied to her, and foisted herself upon Amber's mercy. The woman was a nightmare.

She stood up and looked down at Emilia's sleeping features.

An adorable nightmare.

She shook her head. She was living her worst dream: unemployed, days before Christmas. She needed to get up, get dressed, and go to see the local recruitment consultants. Calling them was a start, but turning up at their doorstep was bound to prove more effective. It wasn't like she had anything else to do to fill her time.

She went into her bedroom and grabbed some clean underwear before entering the bathroom to have a shower.

As the hot water hit her skin, she tried to make sense of the multiple turns the previous day had taken. Arriving at Heathrow in the morning, she had still harboured a tiny hope that she might be able to keep her job. A hope that Bronwyn might have found a speck of Christmas spirit.

Less than five minutes after being fired, Emilia had reappeared in her life. Her evening was supposed to be filled with working on her CV, panicking about employment and money, and counting down the hours until the next work day begun, but Emilia had quickly turned that on its head.

She hadn't had time to think about being unemployed, which had been a blessing. But then she'd spent that time worrying about Emilia. Someone who had a panic attack in a shopping mall was not an ideal candidate to suddenly fly to another country, something that Amber knew she had never done before—planned or not.

Amber turned off the water, stepped out of the shower and wrapped herself up in a fluffy towel. She was looking forward to winter being over, even though she knew the worst had yet to come. January and February would be much colder than it was now. She wondered if she'd be able to afford heating then.

She pushed the thought to one side. She couldn't allow herself to be disheartened. She had to think positively and assume she would get a job, a well-paying, good job. And soon.

She turned on the hairdryer, thankful that the noise of the device was able to drown out her negative thoughts.

She'd become so skilled at her morning routine that a shower, full hair and makeup, and underwear on took just under twenty minutes. Now she needed to raid her wardrobe and decide on clothes. Did she want to dress up in one of her Ted Baker suits, or might that put her out of the running for a lower-paid job that she'd quite happily do on a temporary basis?

She was still thinking about outfits when she opened the bathroom door and saw Emilia standing on the other side of it.

Amber had obviously worn underwear, and far less, in

front of women before, but she still felt a little uncomfortable in such a state of undress with Emilia staring at her.

And she was *staring* at her.

"Um. Are... are you... going out?" Emilia asked, her eyes unashamedly roaming over Amber's body.

She had to admit, she enjoyed the attention. Emilia was obviously not as oblivious as she first appeared.

Amber placed her hands on her hips, casual but still in control. "Yes, I need to look for work. I'm going to hit up some recruitment agencies," she explained.

Emilia licked her lips and dragged her gaze up to meet Amber's.

"Already?"

"Yes, I need to get back into work immediately. I can't afford to be unemployed for more than a couple of days."

"Days?" Emilia balked. "Don't you have savings?"

Amber took a deep breath and reminded herself that Emilia came from another world, one where money arrived in royalty cheques from stories written by her grandmother half a century ago. She had no clue about getting a job or paying bills.

"Not enough. Rent is expensive, everything is expensive. If I don't get back into work soon, I'll lose my home. I'll have to resort to credit cards to get by, and then I'll get into a spiral of debt that will take me a long time to get out of. I pretty much live month to month."

Emilia would have looked more surprised if her eyes hadn't resumed their journey down Amber's torso.

As nice as it was to feel attractive, she had things to do.

"Maybe you could... step aside, so I can get some clothes on?" Amber suggested.

Emilia blushed and quickly moved out of the way.

"Thank you." Amber entered the bedroom and opened her wardrobe. She mentally continued her debate over what to wear. "You're welcome to stay here, of course. I don't know what your plans are."

"Neither do I, yet," Emilia admitted. "I'm still a little shaken up. Thank you, for last night."

Amber stopped and turned around. "For?"

"For cuddling in front of the television. I felt much better, I must have because I fell asleep."

Amber smiled. "You're welcome. As I say, you can stay here if you like. I don't know when I'll be back, though."

"I think I'd like that," Emilia said.

Amber turned to her wardrobe. She decided on a simple black suit, classy and yet middle of the road enough to allow her to apply for any job that was available.

"Great, I'll give you a key and show you how to lock up in case you want to go out. And how to deadbolt the door after I've gone."

She slipped on the skirt and zipped it up, shuffling it around until it was positioned correctly. A white blouse was next, quickly buttoned, with a black jacket thrown over the top. She looked at her reflection in the full-length mirror and was satisfied. Slipping on some heels, she turned to leave the bedroom.

Emilia was still gaping at her. Amber smothered a smile. It was surprisingly pleasurable to be objectified by Emilia. She'd have to investigate this further, at another time when she wasn't in such a hurry.

"There's leftover takeaway from last night, and some

stuff in the cupboards," Amber explained as she walked out of the bedroom. "Help yourself to whatever you find. Which isn't much as I've not had time to go shopping since I got home."

"I'll be fine," Emilia reassured.

"Just… be careful. Don't open the door, even if someone knocks. And if you go out, don't talk to strangers." She stopped when she realised that her extensive safety list would probably terrify Emilia. "You'll be fine. Oh, and help yourself to clothes from my wardrobe if you want to shower or whatever. Just… help yourself to anything."

"Thank you, you're very kind," Emilia said.

She supposed she was. Considering what had happened, she didn't think she ought to be giving Emilia carte blanche to her home and belongings, but the anger she'd been holding onto had slipped away.

She wondered if it had simply been replaced with worry about her job situation, and the anger was still lurking in the background. Although, the warm feeling she got when she looked at Emilia's face told her that probably wasn't the case.

32

EXPLORING

EMILIA SAT on Amber's sofa with a mug of foul-tasting coffee. It had been an hour since Amber left, and she'd not yet felt brave enough to do anything but sit in the living area.

The problem was that she was insanely curious about Amber's home and lifestyle. She didn't want to snoop, but the pull to learn more was extremely strong.

Her gaze drifted towards the bookshelf in the corner. She reasoned that if the books were on display in the living area, then they were safe to look at. She put the mug on the coffee table and bent in front of the shelves. She recognised some of the titles and slid some out of the shelf to look a little closer when she couldn't identify them. A smile touched her lips when she came across a couple of lesbian romance novels.

Guilty pleasure, she reminded herself as she recalled Amber's red-stained cheeks when she had caught her with one.

Emilia had read a few lesbian romances—and gay romances—in her time. As far as she was concerned, love was love. It was only now that she understood that she was a lot more comfortable with the idea than she first thought.

But she was still processing that information.

Along the bottom shelf, she noticed there were a handful of CDs, and then a long row of DVD box sets. She pivoted and looked at the television. Amber seemed to love watching movies and TV shows and knew a lot about them all.

Her hand snatched the remote control off the coffee table. She stared at the buttons, trying to recall how Amber had turned the screen on. She couldn't believe that all the buttons were actually relevant.

After a while she pushed a button that caused the screen to flicker to life. She sat on the sofa, leaning forwards as she flipped through channels. News, weather, movies—both old and new—comedies, science fiction… everything she could imagine flashed by. She supposed she could understand Amber's fascination with the device.

Curling up with her the night before had been lovely. She'd found herself drawn into the fantasy landscape of the movie that Amber had chosen. Though utter exhaustion had eventually sent her to sleep, even now she found herself wondering how the movie had ended.

She'd woken at one point during the night to find Amber almost laying on top of her. She had felt so warm and safe that she'd quickly slipped back to sleep. Finding Amber gone in the morning had been horrible, until she heard the distant sound of a hairdryer and realised where she was.

Her cheeks heated at the thought of seeing Amber in only her black bra and panties that morning. Walking around with such confidence, looking so gorgeous. Emilia knew she should have turned away and given her some privacy, but she couldn't help it. She'd stared and probably embarrassed herself, but she'd do it again if she had another opportunity to see Amber like that.

Emilia had never really given that much thought to her own appearance. Why would she? It was only her most of the time. She showered frequently, got her hair cut every month, she moisturised as it would be impossible to live in a cold climate without doing so. Aside from those basics, she never considered what she looked like.

Amber was different, she took a lot of pride in her appearance.

She leaned back and looked down at herself. Amber had told her that she was welcome to shower and even to pick clothes from her wardrobe. Getting clean and having the chance to freshen up was very appealing. As was taking an—invited—look through Amber's wardrobe.

She correctly guessed the off button, and the television screen faded to black. She rinsed out the mug of terrible coffee, somehow delaying going into the bathroom. Of course, she'd already been in there, but this time she'd be showering. Exactly as Amber had been that morning.

It seemed intimate, which she knew was silly.

After a while she had tidied everything possible in the kitchen and had to make her way into the bathroom. Amber's expensive-smelling perfume hit her immediately.

She looked at the toiletries that lined the shelves, all the lotions and creams that went into Amber's preparation for a day in her world.

She opened a few and sniffed them, feeling naughty as she did. Everything seemed exotic and exciting. Like Amber.

She decided she had to do something nice for Amber that day. It was incredible that she had opened her home to Emilia despite everything that had happened. And now she was unemployed, desperately seeking work. Emilia had no idea what that felt like, but she wasn't so naïve that she didn't understand it was a big deal. Just because she had never had a job herself didn't mean she couldn't comprehend the importance of having one. Especially in a place like London.

She opened the glass shower screen and looked at the taps with a frown. Even that looked like a puzzle in this strange world where Amber dwelled. She pulled, pushed, and twisted various levers and was eventually soaked when a stream of water fell from the ceiling.

She jumped back and shook her arm a few times. Turning around, she closed and then locked the door. It was probably overkill considering the deadbolt on the front door, but she felt altogether safer knowing the bathroom door was also locked.

A thought floated through her mind. She wondered who else had been in the apartment. Who else had showered here? Amber had admitted that she was bisexual, had there been other women here? Men? Emilia shivered. She didn't like the thought of Amber with a lover, whatever the gender.

But it was completely irrelevant. Amber probably hated her. Just because Emilia was realising that her friendship had started in infatuation and quickly turned into something deeper, it didn't make any difference to Amber's feelings.

She shucked out of her wet clothes, determined to start the day and do something nice for Amber.

London was noisy, messy, frantic, and terrifying. Emilia sat in a coffee shop and looked out of the fogged-up window onto the rainy street. The rain didn't bother her, she was used to that in winter in Sweden, but the sheer volume of people on the street had caused her chest to tighten in fear.

She'd taken cover in the first coffee shop she had found, relieved when a good-quality filter coffee had been placed in front of her by a friendly waitress. Now, she blew the steam from the top of the glorious beverage and watched the scene from behind the protection of the glass window.

Some people might have considered hiding out in a coffee shop as a failure, but Emilia was proud of herself. She hadn't run home, which had been her first instinct.

Walking around the neighbourhood had been equal parts fascinating and petrifying. The masses of people were one thing, but on top of that, *everything* was different. She of course had known deep down that that would be the case, but it was as if she'd forgotten that other countries would be different to home.

She'd always been fascinated with the idea of travel. She'd resigned herself to never actually going through with it herself, assuming that she wasn't brave enough. Travel for Emilia Lund was done via the pages of books. She'd travelled the world a hundred times if *reading* about places actually counted.

She knew it didn't count, not really. She'd always thought that she wouldn't be brave enough to step foot on foreign soil.

Until now.

A smile curled on her lip. She was doing it. She was in London, sitting in a coffee shop, watching the world go by —something she would never have pictured herself doing even a week ago.

It might have been the simplest thing in the world for most people, even a daily occurrence, but Emilia felt brave. Like she had conquered some kind of fear, achieved a win over her anxiety.

She wondered if Amber would be proud of her. For some reason, that was important to her. She wanted to tell Amber that she was sitting in a coffee shop, on her own, and everything was fine.

No panic. No worries about crowds, noise, or bright lights. Just a cup of coffee and a view of the rain-soaked street in front of her.

She wondered if Amber ever visited this coffee shop. It was one of the ones nearest to her home. Maybe she had sat in the same seat. Emilia smiled at the connection she suddenly felt to Amber, even if it was imaginary.

Without Amber, she never would have taken this leap into the unknown. She owed the woman a lot, although all she had given her was heartache and stress. Emilia had a plan to try to fix that, to offer her thanks and an apology.

The thought of making Amber happy caused an unexpected smile to brighten her face.

33

DID YOU BUY AN APRON?

AMBER TRIED the lock and felt the weight of the deadbolt holding the door closed. Emilia was home. She wondered if she'd even ventured outside. Part of her hoped she hadn't, London was far too dangerous for someone as trusting as Emilia.

She knocked on the door, hoping that Emilia wasn't some genius squatter who would now claim ownership of her apartment and complete a hat trick of very shitty events.

A few seconds later, the deadbolt shifted, and the door opened.

"Hey!" Emilia grinned.

"Hi," Amber whispered, her attention grabbed by the fact that Emilia was wearing a cooking apron. Amber didn't own a cooking apron.

Did she bring an apron? No, she had no bags… Did she go out and buy one?

She stepped over the threshold and was shocked to realise that Emilia was cooking. She must have been out and bought ingredients—and an apron. It was not what she'd expected at all.

Emilia closed the door behind her.

"You have a lovely market nearby. And your supermarket is huge. There were so many things I've never heard of. But I managed to find all of the ingredients, even if I'd never heard of some of them." Emilia went back to the hob and started stirring ingredients in a frying pan.

"You… went shopping?" Amber dropped her handbag on the table. She couldn't believe that Emilia had been out and was now cooking a meal for her. And had purchased an apron… and was wearing her clothes? She tilted her head to one side. Seeing Emilia from the back she could now see the woman was definitely not wearing the clothes she arrived in.

You did say she could wear your clothes, she reminded herself.

"Yes. And I went to a coffee shop. And I bought some better coffee. The coffee you have is… very weak."

Amber laughed. "Yeah, it's rubbish. I knew you'd hate it."

"I don't hate it," Emilia denied. "I just know there is better coffee available."

"Yeah, yeah. You hate it." Amber took off her jacket and placed it on the back of a dining chair. "What are you making? It smells familiar."

Emilia looked at her nervously, biting her lip.

"What?" Amber asked.

"I hope you don't mind, but I saw a recipe book in the kitchen. I wanted to make you a meal, but I didn't know what you liked. I saw this pork recipe, and the page was very well worn so I assumed it must be a favourite."

Amber smiled. She had expected Emilia to snoop around while she was gone. If the worst she had done was check out her mother's recipe book, then it didn't worry her.

"The pork with broccoli and sesame?" Amber asked.

"Yes. And the sauce, which smells amazing. It has a lot in it, so I hope I'm making it right."

"Smells delicious. You didn't have to do this," Amber told her. She looked around the apartment. Something felt different. "Did you *clean*?"

"Oh, yes, I cleaned the whole apartment. It didn't take long because it's so sm… it was very clean already."

Amber walked around in shock. Everything looked so neat and shiny. Her terrible day was being quickly turned around. She may have been disappointed at every recruitment consultant she went to, especially the last one which had closed early for a Christmas party, but coming home to her favourite meal and a clean apartment was great.

"You really didn't have to do all this," Amber said.

"I know. I wanted to." Emilia focused on the meal.

"And it's adorable that you bought an apron," Amber teased.

"Well, I am wearing your clothes," Emilia pointed out.

"Indeed you are." Amber looked forward to seeing the fitted white blouse on Emilia when the apron came off. She shook her head and turned away. She needed to keep perspective and stop thinking of Emilia in that way, even if she was thrilled about finally seeing her in something other than thick, cosy sweaters.

"Is that okay?" Emilia looked worried. She started to pull at the apron strings. "I can take it off?"

Please, Amber thought. "No, it's fine. It looks good on you."

Emilia blushed. "No, no. You look much better in office wear."

They paused and looked at each other for a moment, each unsure what to say next. The atmosphere was becoming slightly charged, and Amber didn't know what to make of it. Emilia had spent a lot of time staring at her body that morning, but that could probably be explained by Emilia not seeing another female body very often. She was... curious.

Probably.

A little voice in Amber's head suggested that maybe Emilia wasn't just curious.

"Did you have any luck at your meetings?" Emilia asked, thankfully changing the subject.

"No. As I feared, everyone is winding down for Christmas. I need to spend some time online looking for jobs." She winced as she remembered something. "Oh, damn. I can't tonight."

"No?"

"No, I just remembered what day it is. You recall that I volunteer at the local library to read to kids. At first it was a great way to do some market research, you know, speak to kids about books. What better place, right? But then I found I really enjoyed it, so I kept going." She ran a hand through her hair, stressed that her evening with the laptop was slipping through her fingers.

"That sounds like a lot of fun. Maybe I could come along?" Emilia asked.

"Absolutely, it would be great to have some company." For all her work-related anxiety, she was surprised at how quickly she agreed. Surely, she should have wanted Emilia gone? Out of her clothes and her apartment? Back in Sweden and well away from her?

But she didn't. Despite the residual anger still floating around her brain, she wanted Emilia with her.

"I… I'm going to get changed," she said. She'd left the room to get some space before Emilia had the chance to reply.

She sat on the edge of her bed and stared at the floor for a few long moments. She still didn't know exactly what was going on between them. Nothing made sense. Emilia was unlike anyone she'd ever met before, and while that endeared the woman to her, it also made it harder to figure things out.

"I'll talk to her tonight," she muttered to herself. "Finally clear the air."

She had no idea what she was going to say but starting the conversation at all would be a step in the right direction.

34

AT THE LIBRARY

THE LIBRARY WAS a modern building which seemed to incorporate many council services under one roof. Amber had explained how recent council funding cuts had caused many libraries in the UK to be closed, but some had managed to survive and even thrive by being in buildings that combined many things in one place.

It was nothing like the run-down library back home which Emilia knew so well. This building was spacious, warm, and welcoming. There was a café serving hot drinks and cakes. Down one corridor was a doctor's surgery and a pharmacy. Down another corridor were a handful of community spaces to be rented out.

Emilia could easily see the benefits. While councils may struggle to find funding for a library, combining that service with many others was much more financially sound. Especially when some of those services made a profit, like the café.

She liked this approach, especially as it led to a well-stocked library that was filled with children happily running around and begging their parents to be allowed to borrow books.

"This is wonderful," Emilia said.

"It is," Amber agreed. "I've always loved this library. And they have quite a few Walker Clay books in the children's section… donations, I believe." She shrugged innocently and walked further into the library.

Amber had only gone a few steps when two children, a boy and a girl, collided with her legs.

"Amber! Are you reading to us?" the little girl asked.

Emilia felt her heart swell; the children were adorable.

"I am!"

"Yes!" The boy jumped up and down with excitement.

Amber ruffled his hair. "But I don't know what to read, maybe you can get some suggestions?"

Happy with the task, the children rushed off. Emilia could hear them telling their friends that Amber was there and that *they* had been chosen to pick the books. The pride was clear in their tones.

"I usually read two or three books," Amber explained. "Obviously, I do the voices and sound effects and will have to kill you if you mock me later."

Emilia chuckled. "Understood, no mocking. I'm sure you do a wonderful job."

"The kids like it," Amber said.

"I bet, I would have loved this when I was a child," Emilia said.

"Oh, come on." Amber laughed. "You had your grandmother reading her best-selling, award-winning books to you."

"Not as often as I would have liked," Emilia confessed.

It was the first time she had admitted that her childhood was anything less than perfect.

Amber looked confused, but before she could ask anything further, the children were back with handfuls of books. She looked at Emilia apologetically. "I'm sorry… I…"

"It's fine, go. Go." Emilia shooed her away with a smile.

Amber gathered the children into a large circle in the middle of the children's section. Some sat on beanbags, some on tiny chairs, some simply cross-legged on the floor. Amber sat on a small chair which she only just fit on.

A little boy shyly approached her and whispered in her ear. Emilia couldn't hear what he said, but a moment later Amber had nodded and gently positioned the boy on her lap.

Emilia's heart was full to bursting at the endearing scene.

The room grew silent. Amber opened up the hardbacked book and held it in one hand, her other arm wrapped around the boy on her lap. She started to read. Emilia was blown away with the passion that Amber put into the reading. When she'd heard Amber read before, it had been in broken Swedish. In her native language, it was a completely different matter.

Amber was an extremely accomplished reader, pausing in all the right places for extra dramatic emphasis. Her accents made the children, and most of the parents, laugh.

If Emilia had harboured any doubts about her feelings for Amber before, now she knew for certain. She was rapidly falling in love with the impressive woman.

She turned away, needing some space.

She browsed through the children's books, smiling at the bright colours and the weird and wonderful titles. She told herself that she was simply browsing, but in her heart, she knew her eyes were skimming, looking for something familiar.

Eventually, she found it on the bottom shelf. A copy of a Charlotte Lund collection.

She slid the book from the shelf and frowned. It was a little moth-eaten. It looked out of place compared to the other books.

Before she could inspect it further, a little girl rounded the corner at high speed and nearly collided with Emilia, stopping herself moments before impact.

"Sorry," the girl apologised.

"It's okay," Emilia replied.

The girl put a book she was holding back on the shelf. "The library say I have too many books out already," the girl complained.

"How many can you have?" Emilia asked.

"Fifteen."

"That's quite a lot," Emilia said. "You must be a very good reader."

The girl nodded, seemingly happy with the praise.

"I'm sure you'll read your books in no time, and then you can come back and get that one."

"I will," the girl agreed. "But it's okay. I've already read it, it's my favourite book."

"Oh." Emilia picked up the book. It looked bright and fun, with made-up animals on the front. She flipped through, intrigued by the style of the book. It was like nothing she had seen before.

She looked at the girl and held up the collection of her grandmother's stories. "Have you ever read this one?"

The girl looked at it and shook her head. She reached out and took the book from Emilia's hand. She opened it up and leafed through the pages, a frown on her face.

"What do you think of it?" Emilia asked.

"It's okay," the girl said, though it was obvious she was being kind. "But I don't think I'll read it." She handed the book back.

Emilia tried to smile. "Maybe one day when you have read all the other books."

"Maybe," the girl agreed.

Probably not, Emilia thought, judging from her tone.

A woman's voice called out a name in the distance.

"I have to go," the girl said.

"Nice talking to you," Emilia said. She watched the girl leave before looking at the two books in her hands.

They were like night and day in the way they were presented. One was modern with bright colours and drawings made with thick brushstrokes. The other was classic in appearance, the drawings black and white in charcoal sketches with hints of pale watercolours.

She placed the colourful book back on the shelf before crouching down and putting the Lund collection back where she had found it, on the lower shelf. When she stood, she took a step back and took in all of the books at once. Her eyes scanned carefully over the shelves, looking at each book.

Her breath hitched in her chest.

In the distance she could hear Amber's voice as she read to the children. She knew in that moment that no child would ever request the Lund collection, and none of them would hear Amber reading it to them.

She shivered at the thought.

3 5

A JOB OFFER

THE WALK HOME WAS SILENT. Amber knew something was wrong with Emilia but decided to leave her to speak up about whatever it was. She didn't think it was Emilia's anxiety, as she had happily spoken with both children and parents at the library. It was something that had happened during or after the reading. Probably when she vanished from Amber's sight for a while.

Something had Emilia's mind ensnared. Amber could only wait for her to say what it was.

The silence aside, she'd had a lovely night. She hadn't thought it would be possible to have a pleasant night considering the disappointing day. Coming home to her favourite meal, which Emilia had cooked perfectly, and then seeing all the kids and talking to them about Father Christmas had been great.

If she could just sort out her employment situation, things would be perfect.

Until Emilia went home and took with her home-cooked meals, cuddles on the sofa, and appreciative looks when she thought Amber wasn't looking.

They hadn't discussed when Emilia was going home, mainly, if she admitted it, because Amber didn't want to say goodbye. Over the course of the evening, her anger had faded to nothing and been replaced with fondness.

In fact, her anger had been piled, quite rightly, at Bronwyn's door. The woman who'd wanted her gone for months, and the woman who'd given her the impossible task. Bronwyn had used Emilia's reclusive nature against Amber. That wasn't Emilia's fault, all Emilia had ever done was be herself.

And lie, Amber reminded herself. She still didn't know why, but she couldn't imagine the reason was a malicious one. That just didn't fit Emilia's personality.

As much as Amber hated being lied to, it did mean that she got to experience Swedish culture and have some of the most fun she'd had in years. Even if that fun was primarily reading and talking with Emilia.

It wasn't like she'd been on holiday to a theme park or a ski lodge and had fun in a place designed for enjoyment. She'd been to a place where she'd had some truly terrible experiences, and still felt like she had a great time.

She couldn't ignore that that was because of Emilia.

All the best moments were when she was just hanging out with Emilia.

It was hard to align the woman she'd enjoyed spending so much time with, and the woman who had lied to her and caused her stress beyond measure. She found herself in a push-pull mindset. One moment she wanted to sweep Emilia into a tender hug and look after her, the next she wanted to keep her at arm's length because of the trouble she had caused.

They arrived back at the apartment, Emilia pushing the button for the elevator.

"Would you like some foul coffee when we get in?" Amber asked, trying to generate some conversation. "Or maybe some tea? It's harder to ruin that."

"Tea sounds nice," Emilia said. Her gaze was fixed on the doors as something turned in her mind.

They entered the apartment, Emilia dead-bolting the front door like a pro despite her obvious distraction.

Amber made tea while Emilia emptied the dishwasher. Emilia had never seen a dishwasher before, so Amber had shown her how to stack it and turn it on. She was struck by how pleasantly domestic it was as they both went about their respective tasks in companionable silence.

Somehow, she knew that Emilia's thoughts were not anxious or angry, they were contemplative. She also knew that she'd talk about them whenever she was ready.

They sat on the sofa with their tea. Amber reached for the remote control.

"Can we talk?" Emilia asked.

"Sure." She leaned back on the sofa and pivoted herself to face Emilia.

"I'd like you to do something for me." Emilia placed her mug on the coffee table, her fingers knotting together anxiously.

"Which is?" Amber asked.

"I… I realise I've been very selfish," Emilia said. "In more ways than one. You see, I was so consumed by never spoiling my grandmother's books that I think I have condemned them without knowing it."

Amber eyes widened in surprise. She hadn't expected that admission.

"I told you that I would never give my grandmother's books to a faceless corporation, and that's still true. I fear giving control over to people who don't care as much as I do," Emilia said. She stared down at her hands.

"My grandmother had an agent who dealt with these things, Magnus. He worked alongside her and dealt with all of the business and publishing elements. When I took control of the rights, I was so grateful for Magnus because he knew everything that I didn't. He kept the books in a form I could recognise, and they continued to sell."

"I know of Magnus, he's not the easiest to get hold of," Amber said.

"Because I'm selfish," Emilia replied. "He is very old, he doesn't want to work anymore, and I make him because I haven't found anyone else to do the job. He's stuck. Because of me."

Amber couldn't deny the facts. The poor old man was stuck. Many people would have let go of the obligation somehow, but she suspected that a strong work ethic and a relationship with the family that stretched back decades made that impossible for poor Magnus.

"And I'm ruining the books, I'm killing them." Emilia covered her face with her hands as she started to sob.

Amber put her tea mug down and scooted closer. She put her hands on Emilia's knee.

"Hey, no… you're not doing that at all."

"I am," Emilia breathed.

"You're not, the books are fine. They are charting well throughout Scandinavia."

Emilia lowered her hands. Her eyes were red and wild as she looked at Amber.

"Maybe back home, and in our neighbouring countries. But not overseas. Not like they were. I'd convinced myself that sales decline naturally, but they don't. They only do that if you don't keep up with trends. I saw a little girl at the library today, she's an avid reader and had to put a book back because she already had too many out on loan."

Amber plucked a tissue from the nearby box and held it out to Emilia.

"Thank you." She wiped at her tears. "I found a copy of one of the Lund collection. It looked old and torn. Well-loved, but abandoned on the bottom shelf. I asked the girl if she would consider borrowing it, and she said no. When I compared it to the book she had returned to the shelf, they were similar but completely different."

"What do you mean?"

"The stories were similar; most children's stories are when you think about fairy tales and the lessons they aim to teach. But the design was different. The inside was familiar, but the packaging was not."

"Ah." Amber knew exactly what she was referring to. The fact that the Lund books looked their age and most children weren't going to be attracted to that.

"Children want things that are new and exciting," Emilia said. "They don't want things that look old, that's for us adults. We want to hang onto our past, but to children it just looks… boring. And no child will want to pick up the Lund collection unless things change."

"But you need a faceless corporation in order to do that," Amber said.

"No, no." Emilia smiled through her tears. "I need you."

"Me?" Amber sat back in surprise. "What do you mean?"

"I don't understand the business side of publishing. I don't actually think I understand anything about publishing, aside from the books it eventually produces. You do. And you understand what children want. I want you to be my agent. Magnus can finally retire, and I… I promise I will listen to you. I want the Lund collection to live on. I want a child in London to pick up a book and have the same feelings I did when I was a child."

Amber blinked a few times to clear her mind. "You… you know what you're asking, right?"

"I'll pay you, of course. Well, the Lund estate will. It will be a job. A proper job. And I will listen."

Amber held up her hand to stop Emilia's rambling.

"You'll not like what I have to say," Amber warned. "I'll tell you that all of the illustrations need to go. And the titles need to change. I'll want to drop some of the darker stories altogether, even if they have a good meaning to them."

Emilia nodded sadly. "I know, I know. Things cannot remain the same forever."

Amber didn't want to argue with Emilia. Just the thought of trying to convince her which artist to use in the refresh was already giving her a headache.

"I'm not sure if this is a good idea," she confessed.

"But… it has to be you, I don't trust anyone else."

"You need to shop around for an agent, or a publisher, that you like."

"I like you."

"I'm not an agent."

"You could be," Emilia argued.

Amber stood up and looked out of the window. It was true, she could be an agent. She didn't know if she wanted to be one, but it was a job she had some experience with. But working for Emilia… could that work?

Then again, they'd been through a time that could have torn them apart and now they were enjoying tea in Amber's living room. Would arguing with Emilia really be that terrible? It wasn't like she was the sort to throw things, just pout like a puppy who was denied a treat. It was better than working with someone volatile like Bronwyn.

And Emilia wouldn't have to be her only client. Maybe this was a chance to carve out a new career, one where she worked for herself. The idea of being a self-employed agent was exhilarating and terrifying.

Why the hell not? Amber thought to herself. *You know you can do this. And you'll be helping Emilia out, as a friend. The Lund collection deserves to live on.*

"Okay," she said. She turned around from the window and nodded at Emilia.

Emilia blinked. "O-okay? You mean you'll do it?"

"Yes, I'll be your agent."

Emilia jumped up from the sofa and enveloped her in a bear hug. "Thank you, thank you! I promise I will listen to what you have to say. I will remind myself that I want the Lund collection to live on forever and that you can help me to do that."

"I don't make any promises, publishing is a difficult industry," Amber warned.

Emilia leaned back, her arms still loosely around Amber's shoulders. "I know. I know you will do your best, and that's all I can ask."

"I need to know something first," Amber said. "I need to know why you lied to me. Why did you get me to come and stay with you when you had no intention of signing a contract? Or did you think that maybe you would? Has this been bubbling away for a while?"

Emilia lowered her arms and took a step back. She shook her head. "No, I was never going to sign that contract. If you wanted us to go to Walker Clay in the future, I would now have to consider it. But at that time... no."

"Then why did you lie to me?"

Emilia's cheeks flushed a deep red. "I wanted a friend."

Amber's heart broke. "A... friend?"

"Yes. It can't have escaped your notice that I don't have many people in my life. When your letter arrived, Hugo suggested I meet up with you just to have some kind of social interaction with someone. The only person I really speak to is him. I wanted to prove to him that I could talk to other people. And then I met you, and it was so nice and easy to talk to you. I wondered if we'd be friends if we knew each other better, but I knew that you would never be back..."

"Unless you lied about the contract," Amber realised.

"So, you asked me to stay so that... we might end up being friends?"

"Yes. I know that sounds silly. I just... I don't really understand it all myself. Part of me wanted to prove to Hugo that I could make friends, that there was nothing wrong with me and I could socialise just fine without his help."

"And the other part of you?"

"The other part of me wanted you to be my friend," Emilia confessed. "I wanted to prove the same thing to myself, but I knew that lying to you was wrong and it was eating me up. I convinced myself that you would have stayed anyway because you were having such a fun time. I ruined everything."

Amber wanted to be angry about the subterfuge, but how could she be? Emilia was obviously lonely and out of practice when it came to the art of making friends. In some ways Amber felt like she was speaking with a child who knew it was wrong to steal but had done so simply because they were hungry. There was an ethical dilemma, but could she forgive the crime if she understood the motive behind it?

In this case, Amber knew she could. Being angry at Emilia was impossible.

"You didn't ruin everything. I understand," she said.

"You... you do?"

"I do. I don't like the way you went about it, but I understand it," Amber admitted.

"So, I haven't ruined everything?" Emilia looked at her with big doe eyes.

Amber chuckled. "No, you haven't ruined everything. Not at all. I don't think I could ever be mad at you."

Emilia launched forward and hugged Amber again, this time nearly knocking her off her feet. Amber wrapped her arms around her and swayed along with her.

"Thank you, thank you," Emilia said again. "I really thought what I had done was unforgivable."

"It was pretty shitty," Amber confessed, "but I understand you didn't mean harm by it. Your heart was in the right place. And I can't deny that I had a great time being your friend."

Emilia adjusted her position, sliding her cheek along Amber's until her soft lips captured hers. Amber was shocked by the sudden and unexpected kiss, too shocked to respond. Emilia's hands softly touched her cheeks, and she kissed her again.

Amber woke up from her daze, took Emilia's hands, and stepped backwards.

Hurt flashed across Emilia's face.

"I… I don't think this is a good idea," Amber said.

Emilia blushed deeply. "I'm sorry. You're right, I got… swept up. I'm sorry, that was wrong of me. I'll… I'll be flying home tomorrow. I leave at midday. Of course I'll keep my mobile phone on so I can speak to my new agent," she said with a tentative grin. "We can still work together, I hope?"

"Yes, of course. I just—"

"I'm tired, I think I'll go to bed." Emilia turned and all but ran towards the bedroom, slamming the door behind her.

36

A LOT BRAVER THAN YOU THINK

AMBER STARED at the closed door in shock. She couldn't believe that Emilia had kissed her, and she had no idea what it meant. Emilia was unlike anyone Amber had met before, and so analysing her behaviour was practically impossible at times.

She wished she'd reacted better. She stepped away from the kiss because she was worried that they were rushing into things. It was obvious there was a tension between them, but she didn't know if it was a shared tension or if Emilia was picking up on Amber's feelings. The last thing she wanted to do was push Emilia into something she wasn't ready for.

The whole point in stopping the kiss was so she could understand better what Emilia was thinking and make sure that she didn't get hurt. But it appeared that she'd done that anyway.

She groaned and sat on the sofa, her head in her hands. She'd royally messed up.

There's been a lot to process, she reminded herself. *It's been a stressful time.*

There was no way that this wouldn't affect their friendship. A rejected kiss wasn't something that anyone could easily bounce back from. Amber hadn't really meant to reject the kiss. Ordinarily, the idea of sharing a kiss with Emilia would have made her ecstatic. But she needed to be sure. She needed to know what Emilia was thinking and feeling, and how it would affect their new positions, which they also hadn't fully talked about.

Everything was up in the air, and Amber felt like her head was about to explode.

Emilia Lund was a complicated woman to figure out. That fact wasn't helped by the fact that Amber knew she had feelings for her. Somewhere, buried in the fascination, anger, and general confusion, lurked fondness. And more, if she were honest with herself.

She touched her lips and closed her eyes, reliving the moment and wishing she'd reacted differently. All she wanted to do was check they were on the same page and make sure they moved slowly as things were changing so fast. If she'd not been so shocked and had been able to react better, she'd still be kissing Emilia.

The door clicked. She lowered her hand and snapped her head up to see a very embarrassed Emilia in the doorway.

"I am very sorry for kissing you like that," Emilia whispered.

Amber stood up. She wrung her hands, desperately not wanting to ruin this second chance she had been bestowed. "There's no need to apologise, I enjoyed the kiss. I just didn't know if it was the right time. A lot of things have happened recently, and I didn't want you to be overwhelmed."

Emilia looked surprised for a moment before folding her arms. "I wasn't overwhelmed. I'm a lot braver than you think I am."

Ooookay, Amber thought. *I didn't expect that reaction.*

She raised an eyebrow in amusement. "I see."

"Yes, in fact, I went out today and sat in a coffee shop. In London."

Amber bit her lip to prevent any retaliatory remarks. Humour was probably not a safe choice right now.

"Well, that's—"

"I'm not some inexperienced… girl. I've travelled to another country," Emilia said, her voice rising as she took a few steps into the room.

"You did, you absolutely did," Amber agreed. "I'm sorry, I didn't mean it to come out like that."

"I've been kissed before, you know," Emilia continued. "I'm not *that* naïve. I'm sure you think you know so much about me… but you don't."

"You're absolutely right," Amber agreed, still trying to not smile at Emilia's sudden surge of argument. From an apology for kissing her to a rousing defence of her experience in a few seconds. God, she loved that Emilia kept her on her toes.

"I'm sorry," Amber tried again. "I just meant that things are moving very quickly. Two weeks ago, we didn't know each other. Then I was practically living with you, then we fought, I came home, got fired—"

"And then I turned up at your office, to end up staying

with you," Emilia added, nodding her head in understanding.

"And now we're working together. It's a lot to take in. Adding that kiss—which was amazing, by the way—into the mix? It's just a little much, too soon."

She noted that Emilia's eyes narrowed at that.

"For me," Amber clarified quickly.

Emilia's expression softened as understanding sunk in. "Oh… I see. I didn't think about it like that. Well, I didn't think about it much at all. It was an impulse," she explained.

"One I appreciated a lot," Amber said. "Just not one I was expecting. I feel like so much as happened lately. I honestly don't know if I'm coming or going. I don't want to make a terrible mistake and ruin everything."

Emilia took a few steps into the room. She was smiling. Amber breathed out a relieved sigh. Maybe things could be fixed?

"I understand," Emilia said. "There has been a lot of change for you. Maybe the… the kiss is something we can talk about later?"

"I'd like that a *lot*," Amber emphasised. "But right now, I'm so stressed and exhausted. I just want to chill out in front of the television. It's my thing, it's how I relax."

Emilia looked at the television. "Maybe you can introduce me to one of your much-talked-about box sets? Unless you want to be alone?"

"I don't want to be alone," Amber said, already looking forward to snuggling up on the sofa with Emilia. "But I will only watch television with you if we can heat up the tea and crack open the biscuits."

"Is there any other way to watch television?" Emilia asked with a grin.

37

FLYING HOME

Emilia woke up with a painfully stiff neck. The pain was quickly forgotten when she realised they had fallen asleep on the sofa again. This time, she was leaning against the arm of the sofa, and Amber was curled up against her chest.

Pain in the neck aside… it felt heavenly.

The urge to wrap her arms around Amber and apply soft kisses to her hair was strong, but she held back. Amber wasn't ready. Perhaps neither of them was.

After the library reading the night before, Emilia had done a lot of soul-searching and realised a few things about herself and about the Lund collection. First, she was a lot braver than she thought she was. Secondly, the world hadn't ended when she pushed herself outside of her comfort zone. And, thirdly, the Lund collection was stuck in the past and would continue to diminish if she didn't take action.

The thought of her grandmother's legacy withering to nothing under her watch was horrifying. Her fear of ruining the books had come true but only through her lack of momentum. Not doing anything was having the same effect as potentially doing the wrong thing, something she never would have realised unless she was pushed out of her shell.

She hadn't asked Amber to be her agent simply because she was the only person she knew who could do such a thing. Nor had she asked her to further trap them together in the vague hope of friendship. She'd asked Amber because she knew she was the right person for the job. She understood the market, and they were close enough now that they could discuss, and even disagree, on matters.

Buoyed by her sudden bravery, and the feeling of Amber in her arms, her perfume in the air… she'd taken a leap and kissed her. A huge mistake. The rebuff had stung. She'd run from the situation and wondered if she had ruined everything. Would Amber want to work for someone who kissed her out of the blue? Could it be construed as harassment?

Last night her midday flight had seemed like a lifetime away, and now she wished it would never come. She was existing in a grey area between wanting to be home and wanting to be with Amber.

But she understood that Amber needed time.

Emilia was ready to dive into whatever Amber would offer her, friendship or more. She felt starved of social interaction and was willing to be whatever Amber wanted her to be.

However, she also knew that Amber had experienced a huge amount of turmoil and stress in the last few days and was busy processing what it all meant. It was up to Emilia to give her the time and space she needed, even if it was the last thing she wanted to do.

Amber woke up and quickly moved herself away from Emilia.

"Sorry," she mumbled.

"No problem," Emilia replied.

She wanted to say more, but she didn't know what that would be.

She was struck by how complicated social interaction could be. Spending all those years alone in her farmhouse suddenly made a lot of sense. She rarely had moments where she didn't know what to say, mainly because there was hardly ever anyone to speak to.

Amber got up and said she was going to use the bathroom to get ready. Emilia nodded, stayed on the sofa, and watched her depart. She wished things could be easier, or that she could order a manual that would tell her exactly what to say and when.

She supposed things would work themselves out in the end, but she didn't like the present uncertainty. She'd finally understood her attraction to Amber, and now she never wanted to let her go.

She took a deep breath, shrugging off the thought. It wasn't for her to make demands on Amber and her feelings. The guilt of her dragging Amber to Sweden under false pretences sat on her chest like a heavy stone. She'd never make that mistake again. Now she would give Amber the time and space she needed and hope that eventually she would come to her of her own accord.

All too soon, they were on the way to the airport. Amber had insisted on accompanying Emilia to Heathrow, something which Emilia was very grateful for. She didn't wish for another awkward taxi journey.

The morning had been quiet, each slightly embarrassed about their second evening of falling asleep on the sofa and waking up in an embrace.

Despite Amber's reassurances that they would talk later —nothing was said.

Emilia wanted to talk about and ignore the upcoming conversation in equal measure. She wondered if Amber had only said that she'd enjoyed the kiss to let her down gently. Perhaps she was eager to get the unstable woman out of her apartment and her life.

The very thought caused a pain in Emilia's chest.

"Which terminal are you leaving from?" Amber asked.

Emilia turned to look at her in confusion. She realised that Amber wouldn't be able to see her expression as she was too busy driving.

"Sorry?"

"Your terminal, there are five of them," Amber added.

"I don't know. I fly with Scandinavian Airlines."

"Probably Terminal Three, then," Amber decided.

Emilia didn't have a clue. She wondered if she would have ever managed to get home without Amber's help. The thought niggled at her. Not the part about needing Amber's help, she wasn't above admitting when she needed assistance, but she did find it frustrating that she didn't know things that were probably obvious to others.

She knew she lived in her own world, one which was safely carved out of all the things she loved and that made her feel safe. Deep down, though, she knew it was unhealthy for her. It had only been a handful of years, and already she couldn't recognise the world around her.

And her solitary lifestyle had damaged her grandmother's legacy. She was working to fix it but wondered if it was too late.

She licked her lips and turned to look at Amber again. She had to tell her, had to explain. It was the first time she had ever had to put it into words, but if she didn't then she felt she would break apart. It was bubbling within her and about to burst out.

"My grandmother died when I was eleven," Emilia said. "The next year, my father was diagnosed with cancer. It didn't take long to claim him, and soon after that, my mother passed away. She couldn't cope with so much loss so quickly. I was raised by my grandfather, but he was… cold and didn't know anything about children. He tried his best. Then, when I finished school, he was old and needed me to help care for him. After he died, I just stopped leaving the house. Well, I think I stopped living."

It felt good to get it out. To finally lift the weight off her shoulders and share it with someone else, even if she now felt guilty about putting that weight onto Amber's shoulders.

"You don't need to say anything," Emilia added quickly. "I just… wanted to let you know. In fact, I'd rather you didn't say anything. I don't know if I'm ready to talk about it further."

Amber took one hand from the steering wheel and placed it on Emilia's own which rested on her leg.

"Whenever you *are* ready, I'll be there for you. That's what friends are for."

Emilia turned her hand over and gently squeezed Amber's.

Even if Amber wanted nothing more than friendship and a working relationship, that would be enough. Amber wasn't just a new friend. She was the start of a new life. Emilia was determined to start to move out of her comfort zone and into the real world.

Even if the thought terrified her.

38

TRYING TO SAY GOODBYE

AMBER'S LEGS felt like they were made of lead. She walked down the long corridors of the airport towards security. Emilia walked beside her, staring around at the bright, wide corridor with wide eyes.

She'd woken up in Emilia's arms, and she couldn't remember the last time she had felt so safe and happy. The shock of that had caused her to rush into the bathroom to get some distance.

How Emilia had become so important to her so quickly was a mystery.

They'd gotten ready to go to the airport in quiet companionship, speaking only when necessary. The realisation that something had changed between them was thick in the air. She wanted to talk to Emilia, to see where they stood and what they both felt, but Emilia had pulled away. Amber feared that she regretted her actions from the night before.

And so, she had remained silent as she drove them to the airport.

Up until Emilia dropped the potted history of her terrible early teens. Amber couldn't imagine such grief and loss in such a short space of time. Not to mention at such a sensitive age. Emilia had been old enough to know what was happening, but too young to have developed healthy coping mechanisms.

She'd wanted to swerve onto the hard shoulder and sweep Emilia into a solid hug. Luckily, she hadn't. Emilia was obviously still processing what had happened, and the influences those events had brought into her life.

She hoped that one day Emilia would be ready to talk. More so, she hoped Emilia would be ready to talk to her. Because she wanted to be Emilia's friend. If she could have nothing more than friendship, it would suffice.

As the security area came into view, her legs felt impossibly heavier. She didn't know how she would say farewell to Emilia as if she were unaffected. She was anything but.

She didn't want to say goodbye. She wanted to hold her close and figure out how this delightful woman had wormed her way into her heart.

"Is this where we must say goodbye?" Emilia asked.

"Yes, I can't go any farther." Amber tapped the boarding pass in Emilia's hand. "Remember to look at the screens for that flight number. They will tell you which gate you need to go to."

"I know. I flew here, remember?" Emilia teased.

"Yes, but Heathrow is a lot bigger. And it's a couple of days before Christmas, so it will be very busy," Amber told her.

Emilia shrugged. "Not on my flight. The travel agent told me there were plenty of seats."

"At Scandinavian Airlines prices, I'm not surprised," Amber joked.

They stood and looked at one another, neither wanting to say goodbye.

"I'm sorry for causing havoc," Emilia suddenly blurted.

Amber burst out laughing. "You certainly did do that. But I'm so glad you did."

"Me too. But I promise I won't do it again." A smile curled at Emilia's lips. "Or maybe…"

Amber swatted her arm. "You better not. Especially now I'm working for you."

"Will this make me your boss?" Emilia asked, a devilish glint in her eye.

"I wouldn't put it like that," Amber said. "More like… partners."

"But I will be paying you, so surely…" Emilia trailed off with a grin.

"Oh, in which case, I'll have to turn your kind job offer down." Amber slowly turned around.

"No, wait!" Emilia grabbed her arm and turned her back to face her. "I'm sorry. I do need you. You will be the boss."

"How about partners?" Amber asked again.

Emilia nodded. "That sounds good." She sighed. "I'm going to miss you."

"I'm going to miss you, too. But I have your number now, so I can text you. As long as I don't send any emojis." She winked.

"Ha-ha." Emilia rolled her eyes. "Maybe I will get a new phone. One that has the Internet."

"That's very 2005 of you."

They shared a sad laugh. The teasing was just a delay in the inevitable goodbye that they both knew was looming.

Amber opened her arms. Emilia walked into the hug and wrapped her arms tightly around her.

"I'm going to miss you so much," Amber admitted.

She was relieved she was in a strong embrace as she worried if her legs would hold her.

"I don't want to go," Emilia admitted.

"I don't want you to go."

Emilia tightened her grip, her fists grabbing at handfuls of Amber's coat. Amber closed her eyes, willing the tears away.

I'm just emotional, she reminded herself. *It's been a rough few days…*

She recalled the kiss from the night before. Soft, eager lips willing hers to respond. She wanted to scream at herself for not returning the gesture, for missing the opportunity.

Emilia loosened her grip, preparing to step away.

Amber couldn't think of anything she wanted less in that moment. She pulled Emilia closer to her, angling her head down to capture her lips. It wasn't a sweet and gentle kiss like the one before. It was insistent, messy, and needy. She didn't want to say goodbye. She didn't want to say anything. Everything she wanted to express was in the kiss.

And—thankfully—Emilia responded in kind. Amber was almost surprised with the wildness of the returned kiss. She quickly recovered and reciprocated. Lips and tongues became a blur.

She was distantly aware of people walking around them. The men and women at the security desks were probably getting an eyeful. But she couldn't find it within herself to care.

It was only when she realised Emilia was swaying, maybe due to lack of oxygen, that she pulled away. They disentangled their arms from one another and stepped back. Emilia looked embarrassed but satisfied. Amber couldn't help but grin.

"You… you better go, before we lose track of time and you miss your flight," she said.

"I'll call you as soon as I get home," Emilia promised. "Merry Christmas, Amber."

She reached up and pressed a small kiss to her cheek.

"God Jul," Amber said in what she thought was mangled Swedish.

It seemed not to matter, as Emilia beamed happily. She turned around and looked towards the security desks.

"I better…"

"Yes."

"I'll call you," she repeated.

"I'll be waiting," Amber promised.

Emilia turned and walked towards security. Amber waited and watched her show her passport and disappear around a corner. She let out a long sigh and slowly turned around.

If her legs had been heavy before, they were like jelly now. And the breath was missing from her lungs. She felt bereft. It seemed impossible that someone could become such an essential part of her survival in such a short space of time. Surely that kind of connection was concocted by storytellers, not for the real world?

It was obvious that she would be unable to get to the car park in this state, never mind drive home. She sat down on a bench and stared at the shiny floor, the reflection of travellers and luggage trolleys passing by at speed.

She'd never felt so weak before. Was this what saying goodbye to someone you cared about felt like? A terrible faintness spreading through her entire body? She felt like all her symptoms would vanish if she could just get to the other side of security and see Emilia again. As if she were the cure to the sudden sickness that had taken control of her.

She slumped in her seat, running her hand through her hair and taking a deep breath. Something dug into her side. She adjusted her jacket, realising that something in the pocket was being pressed into her ribs.

Her fingers grazed the item to move it. Her eyes widened. Her legs no longer felt weak. With her new purpose, she jumped to her feet, knowing what she needed to do.

39

FLYING HOME

EMILIA LEANED her head on the window and watched as the men below the plane manhandled luggage. She was suddenly very glad she hadn't brought any. The cases were being tossed from a tiny truck to a conveyor belt in a way that Emilia was sure wouldn't do the contents any good.

But still she stared at the events unfolding below her. Anything to distract from the pain in her chest at having to be parted from Amber. She didn't know how she'd had the strength to walk away. Everything inside her was saying that she should stay.

She couldn't. She couldn't impose herself on Amber's kindness anymore. She had to leave and go back home.

Even if home suddenly felt different.

For the first time in her adult memory, Emilia felt as if home was somewhere she didn't *have* to be. It was a surprising feeling. She had always assumed she wanted to stay home because she felt safe there. Now it was becoming clearer to her that she stayed because she felt she *had* to be there.

Finally admitting what had happened to rip her perfect family apart had opened up parts of Emilia that she hadn't thought about in many years. She recalled rushing home from school to look after her grandfather as he became increasingly frailer.

When he had died, and she was completely alone, she'd felt the weight of responsibility bear down on her shoulders with a ferocious weight. It was her duty to keep her grandmother's legacy alive and to manage the Lund home to the best of her ability. Even if she was still practically a child.

It was unfair, but she had had no one to explain that to. So, she'd got on with her designated role, all the while burying her feelings about the unjust situation. Who was she to complain? She was alive and healthy. That was more than could be said for her beloved family.

The floodgates were opening. Things that she never thought about, or spoke about, were bubbling to the surface. It was as if the suspended animation she had been in was finally beginning to crack and she was able to process what had happened.

She felt relief. As if she were waking up from a very long sleep. Which she supposed grief was.

"Is this seat taken?" someone asked.

"No," Emilia murmured, still staring at the poor luggage being battered around below the plane.

"Then I'll sit here."

The person sat beside her.

"Okay," Emilia agreed.

"Unless you'd like for me to leave?"

It took a few moments for Emilia to realise what was happening.

I know that voice, she thought. *Can it really be?*

She slowly turned, hoping that her ears were not playing tricks on her.

"Amber!" She looked around the cabin wildly, expecting it to be some kind of joke or illusion.

"Yes, but don't tell anyone. I'm supposed to be in 27A." Amber grinned. "Oh, I hope you can lend me some clothes when we get there, I forgot to pack a bag."

"You're here!" Emilia dragged her into a hug. "You're actually here."

"I couldn't say goodbye."

"You… you paid for a flight?" Emilia leaned back and stared at Amber in shock.

"Yep. And, wow, do Scandinavian Airlines know how to charge for a last-minute flight."

"I'll pay you back," Emilia decided immediately.

"No need, I have a new job. My boss pays me well." Amber winked.

"You're… you're really here?" Emilia still couldn't believe it.

"I am. I haven't worn this coat since I came back from Sweden, it still has my passport in it. And then I thought, 'Why not?'"

Emilia grabbed hold of Amber's hand tightly, fearful to let go.

"Seriously, I either need to borrow some clothes or go to the mall." Amber laughed. "I've never boarded a plane with just my passport, keys, and purse before. You're a bad influence on me, Emilia Lund." She leaned in, placing a sweet kiss on Emilia's lips.

"I am. A terrible influence," Emilia agreed. "And you can borrow my clothes. Or we can go to the mall. I can, I'm brave now."

Amber chuckled. "We'll see. We don't want to use all your bravery up so soon. Besides, I might like searching through your wardrobe as much as you did mine."

"I think I'd like that," Emilia admitted. "But I will need to go to the mall anyway. Maybe you can drive us?"

Amber looked at her in surprise. "Sure, if that's what you want."

"That is what I want." Emilia wrapped her hands around Amber's upper arm and held on, afraid if she let go that she might wake up from the nicest dream she'd had in a long time.

"And what are we buying at the mall?" Amber asked in a whisper, obviously not wanting to break the mood.

"You'll see," Emilia said. The smile broke out in a shiver on her face. "I'm very glad you're here."

"I'm very glad I'm here, too." Amber brought her hand up to place it over Emilia's. "You do indeed cause havoc, but I think I like it."

40

MERRY CHRISTMAS

Hugo stopped dead in his tracks as soon as he saw Amber standing on the porch to greet him. He looked uncertain, trying to peek around Amber in search of Emilia.

"Hej," he said carefully.

"Hi. I'm so glad you could make it." Amber stood to one side and gestured for him to enter the house.

He smiled hesitantly as he passed her and entered the entrance hall. Amber kicked off the untied boots she had borrowed from Emilia and waited while Hugo took off his boots, coat, scarf, and gloves.

"God Jul," she said, trying to break the ice.

"God Jul," he replied, still a little uncertain.

"Look, Hugo, I'm sorry about what happened the last time we met," Amber started. She didn't want there to be a negative atmosphere, on Christmas Day of all days. Well, Christmas Eve. Which was like Christmas Day in Sweden, apparently.

Their last meeting hadn't gone so well, but they were

going to be seeing a lot of each other and so she needed to iron things out.

"I'm the one who should apologise," he said. "I shouldn't have said anything, and I really shouldn't have said what I did say."

"It all worked out for the best, in the end," she reassured him.

He hopped on one foot, keeping his one remaining boot off the clean floor.

"It did?" he asked. "Things are… good?"

"Yes, things are very good," she said. "Even better now you're here. Emilia has some things she wants to show you."

He raised an eyebrow, but Amber didn't say anything else. She walked past him and into the house.

"Are you sure I can't help with anything?" she asked Emilia, who was busily tending to several saucepans and checking on things in the oven.

"I'm sure that you are no help in the kitchen at all," Emilia chuckled at her own quip. "Where is Hugo?"

"Getting his boots off, give him a minute," Amber admonished lightly. She knew Emilia was very excited to see him and to show off a few new additions to the house. It was clear that Emilia enjoyed proving herself to people. Whenever she did something new or something she considered brave she couldn't wait to tell Amber or text Hugo.

Amber presumed that was due to Emilia not having much faith in herself, something that seemed to be slowly changing.

"Sorry, new boots." Hugo entered the kitchen and swept Emilia into a big hug.

Amber felt a spark of jealousy but quickly pushed it back down. Hugo was Emilia's best friend, she needed to get used to that. And the endless talking about Hugo. And the fact that they were apparently huggers.

Who hugged for a very long time.

She cleared her throat and Hugo sprang back.

Emilia didn't seem to notice. She grabbed his hand and led him from the kitchen towards the living area.

"Look," she instructed.

Hugo looked around in confusion until his eyes settled on the television screen. He looked at Emilia in surprise. "A TV? Nice!"

"Yes, I watch TV now," she told him.

"Good, I have a lot of shows to recommend to you," he replied. He turned to face Amber. "You are a very good influence on her."

"That's nothing," Amber said. "Check your phone."

He frowned but got his phone out of his pocket and stared at it blankly for a moment.

"Wi-fi?" He almost cried. He looked up at Amber. "She's *online*?"

"*She* is right here," Emilia said. Something caught her attention in the kitchen, and she hurried off to deal with it.

"She is online. She has an email address now," Amber said.

He looked impressed. "You work fast. You've been here, what, three days?"

"Yes, but I didn't do anything," Amber admitted.

"Emilia wanted to get a television and enable the wi-fi on the phone line. I just drove the car and helped her with the technical details."

He regarded her for a few moments, a touch of a smile in his expression. He stepped closer to her.

"You will be good to her, yes?" he asked.

Amber tried to cover her smirk at the attempted cold glare he was giving her. Attempted because he looked terrified of her. She knew from Emilia that Hugo was very gentle and afraid of his own shadow. The fact that he was trying to intimidate Amber was quite amusing.

But also very sweet. He cared about Emilia, that much was abundantly clear.

"I assure you, I want what is best for Emilia," she whispered back.

"What are you two whispering about?" Emilia asked from the kitchen area.

"I'm offering Hugo a drink," Amber called back. She leaned in and whispered to him again, "I know how special Emilia is. Trust me, I'm going to do everything I can to make her happy."

His frame loosened in relief, and he nodded. "Good, she deserves that."

"Stop whispering," Emilia demanded of both of them. "I know you're talking about me, you know."

Amber had never experienced Christmas in any country other than Britain, so it was a bit of a culture shock to be celebrating Christmas on the twenty-fourth of December, with no turkey, listening to two Swedes singing something that resembled a pirate's sea shanty to her ears.

"So, Santa doesn't come down the chimney here?" Amber asked once they finished singing and drinking some foul-looking liquid which she'd declined based on a quick sniff test.

"No, he comes to your house," Hugo said.

"How does he get in?" Amber asked.

"Through the door," Emilia replied. "And he comes during the day, so the children see him."

Amber lowered her wine glass and placed her hand over Emilia's. "Sweetheart, I don't know how to tell you this… but Santa isn't real."

Emilia gasped playfully. "Don't say such things, you know that Santa is real. And his name is Tomten."

"People dress up as him," Hugo explained as he played with the decorative floral centrepiece. "I dress up and visit my niece."

"That's really weird," Amber said.

"And a strange man who breaks into children's houses in the middle of the night while they are sleeping is perfectly normal, I suppose?" Emilia asked.

Amber opened her mouth to reply but realised she had nothing to say. She'd always just accepted that Santa was a magical old man who delivered presents, somehow squeezing down the chimney and stealing food and booze from the mantelpiece before leaving gifts and going to the next house. Now that she thought about it, that seemed very strange and dark. Maybe the Swedish way was better.

"You both have to eat more," Emilia instructed.

Hugo abandoned the centrepiece and stood up. He

grabbed his dinner plate and hurried over to the kitchen where enough food to feed twenty people sat in a buffet style.

"I'm going to need a little bit of digesting time," Amber said.

"Okay, but you must try the herring."

"I'm not trying the herring." Amber shook her head. It was another thing that had failed the sniff test.

"What if I offered you a kiss?" Emilia asked teasingly.

"I don't want to kiss a herring." Amber winked.

"You are impossible." Emilia smiled as she snatched up her dinner plate and went to the kitchen for second helpings.

"When are you going home, Amber?" Hugo asked.

"I don't know yet," she admitted.

They hadn't spoken about it. Since she had arrived they had studiously avoided the topic of when she would leave again. It was obvious that she would have to at some point, but with Christmas looming so close, neither wanted to consider spending the holidays without the other.

She noticed Emilia looking at her nervously.

"I don't have to work and I'm having a great time here, so I'll stay as long as I'm welcome," she said, staring directly at Emilia as she did.

Emilia looked visibly relieved.

"Good. Maybe you can both come to Copenhagen with me for New Year's Eve?" Hugo suggested.

"Yes, I think we'd like that," Emilia said.

Hugo looked stunned, as if he had asked on a whim but assumed that the answer would be no. Amber filed away a mental note to speak to Emilia about it more later. While Emilia kept claiming that she was 'braver now', Amber didn't want her to go too far too soon.

Things were still up in the air for both of them, they were still navigating what their new relationship meant. Discussions had taken place regarding Amber's new status as the agent to the Lund collection, and agreements had been made. She'd take over the role with immediate effect after Christmas was over and they could speak with Magnus.

Amber had a hundred ideas for ways to rejuvenate the books, and plenty to speak about with Emilia when the time was right. In the meantime, she was far more interested in getting to know Emilia on a personal level.

They'd spoken about what they both were feeling, the consensus being that they were falling hard for one another. Amber couldn't believe that she had been unable to find the perfect partner for her in the city of London but had found who she strongly believed to be the one in a small town in Sweden.

Fate, she kept telling herself. *Or maybe a Christmas miracle.*

"Eat more food," Emilia whispered in her ear as she sat back down at the dining table.

"I will, I'm just preoccupied," Amber admitted.

"By?"

"Realising how lucky I am," she said. "And how this is the best Christmas ever."

Emilia leaned in and kissed her softly on the lips. It was much tamer than the kiss they had shared before Hugo's arrival, Amber noted with a grin.

"You say the sweetest things," Emilia told her.

Amber picked up her wine glass and gestured for Emilia to do the same.

"To us," Amber toasted.

"Merry Christmas," Emilia said.

"God Jul," Amber replied, and they clinked their glasses together.

PATREON

I adore publishing. There's a wonderful thrill that comes from crafting a manuscript and then releasing it to the world. Especially when you are writing woman loving woman characters. I'm blessed to receive messages from readers all over the world who are thrilled to discover characters and scenarios that resemble their lives.

Books are entertaining escapism, but they are also reinforcement that we are not alone in our struggles. I'm passionate about writing books that people can identify with. Books that are accessible to all and show that love—and acceptance—can be found no matter who you are.

I've been lucky enough to have published books that have been best-sellers and even some award-winners. While I'm still quite a new author, I have plans to write many, many more novels. However, writing, editing, and marketing books take up a lot of time… and writing full-time is a treadmill-like existence, especially in a very small niche market like mine.

Don't get me wrong, I feel very grateful and lucky to

be able to live the life I do. But being a full-time author in a small market means never being able to stop and work on developing my writing style, it means rarely having the time or budget to properly market my books, it means immediately picking up the next project the moment the previous has finished.

This is why I have set up a Patreon account. With Patreon, you can donate a small amount each month to enable me to hop off of my treadmill for a while in order to reach my goals. Goals such as exploring better marketing options, developing my writing craft, and investigating writing articles and screenplays.

My Patreon page is a place for exclusive first looks at new works, insight into upcoming projects, Q&A sessions, as well as special gifts and dedications. I'm also pleased to give all of my Patreon subscribers access to **exclusive short stories** which have been written just for patrons. There are tiers to suit all budgets.

My readers are some of the kindest and most supportive people I have met, and I appreciate every book borrow or purchase. With the added support of Patreon, I hope to be able to develop my writing career in order to become a better author as well as level up my marketing strategy to help my books to reach a wider audience.

https://www.patreon.com/aeradley

ABOUT THE AUTHOR

Amanda Radley had no desire to be a writer but accidentally became an award-winning, bestselling author.

She gave up a marketing career in order to make stuff up for a living instead. She claims the similarities are startling.

She describes herself as a Wife. Traveller. Tea Drinker. Biscuit Eater. Animal Lover. Master Pragmatist. Procrastinator. Theme Park Fan.

Connect with Amanda
www.amandaradley.com

FITTING IN

2020 Amazon Kindle Storyteller Finalist

Starting a new job is hard. Especially if you're the boss's daughter

Heather Bailey has been in charge of Silver Arches, the prestigious London shopping centre, for several years. Financial turmoil brings a new investor to secure the future and Heather finds herself playing office politics with the notoriously difficult entrepreneur Leo Flynn. Walking a fine line between standing her ground and being willing to accept change, Heather has her work cut out for her.

When Leo demands that his daughter is found a job at Silver Arches; things become even harder.

Scarlett Flynn has never fit in. Not in the army, not in her father's firm, not even in her own family. So starting work at Silver Arches won't be any different, will it?

A heartwarming exploration of the art of fitting in.

GOING UP

2020 Selfies Finalist

A ruthless executive. A destitute woman. Both on the way up.

Selina Hale is on her way to the top. She's been working towards a boardroom position on the thirteenth floor for her entire career. And no one is going to get in her way. Not her clueless boss, her soon to be ex-wife, and most certainly not the homeless person who has moved into the car park at work.

Kate Morgan fell through the cracks in a broken support system and found herself destitute. Determined and strong-willed, she's not about to accept help from a mean business woman who can't even remember the names of her own nephews.

As their lives continue to intertwine, they have no choice but to work together and follow each other on their journey up.

SECOND CHANCES

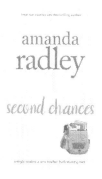

Bad childhood memories start to resurface when Hannah Hall's daughter Rosie begins school. To make matters more complicated, Hannah has been steadfastly ignoring the obvious truth that Rosie is intellectually gifted and wise beyond her years.

In the crumbling old school she meets Rosie's new teacher Alice Spencer who has moved from the city to teach in the small coastal town of Fairlight.

Alice immediately sees Rosie's potential and embarks on developing an educational curriculum to suit Rosie's needs, to Hannah's dismay.

Teacher and mother clash over what's best for young Rosie.

Will they be able to compromise? Will Hannah finally open up to someone about her own damaged upbringing?

And will they be able to ignore the sparks that fly whenever they are in the same room?

Printed in Great Britain
by Amazon